YO-BDE-586

BEYOND LOVE

THE HUTTON FAMILY BOOK 2

ABBY BROOKS

MAIN LIBRARY
Champaign Public Library
200 West Green Street
Champaign, Illinois 61820-5193

Connect with
ABBY BROOKS

WEBSITE:

www.abbybrooksfiction.com

FACEBOOK:

http://www.facebook.com/abbybrooksauthor

FACEBOOK FAN GROUP:

https://www.facebook.com/
groups/AbbyBrooksBooks/

TWITTER:

http://www.twitter.com/xo_abbybrooks

INSTAGRAM:

http://www.instagram.com/xo_abbybrooks

BOOK+MAIN BITES:

https://bookandmainbites.com/abbybrooks

Want to be one of the first to know about new releases, get exclusive content, and exciting giveaways? Sign up for my newsletter on my website:

www.abbybrooksfiction.com

And, as always, feel free to send me an email at: abby@abbybrooksfiction.com

Books by

ABBY BROOKS

Brookside Romance

Wounded

Inevitably You

This Is Why

Along Comes Trouble

Come Home To Me

Wilde Boys Series with Will Wright

Taking What Is Mine

Claiming What Is Mine

Protecting What Is Mine

The Moore Family Series

Blown Away (Ian and Juliet)

Carried Away (James and Ellie)

Swept Away (Harry and Willow)

Break Away (Lilah and Cole)

Purely Wicked (Ashley & Jackson)

Love Is...

Love Is Crazy (Dakota & Dominic)

Love Is Beautiful (Chelsea & Max)

Love Is Everything (Maya & Hudson)

Immortal Memories

Immortal Memories Part 1

Immortal Memories Part 2

As Wren Williams

Bad, Bad Prince

Woodsman

FOREWORD

Family is a strong theme in all of my books. As is growth and learning to love yourself for who you are, flaws and all.

In some of my other series, the family itself is damn near flawless, and the only things my characters have to overcome are their own weaknesses and misguided beliefs.

That's not true for the Huttons.

In this series, I want to explore not only the growth of the characters, but also the healing of the family after their father's death. When I came to the end of book one, I realized that in order to really explore the healing, I needed to look at the sickness itself.

While Burke Hutton started out as the perfect image of a father, he fell into alcoholism and slowly devolved into the kind of man that rattled his family to pieces instead of bringing them together.

What was it like to grow up with a man like that as a father?

What scars did it leave on the family, and how can they honestly move forward without spreading the rot he planted in their hearts?

Wyatt's story starts before his father's death—which was where book one picked up. In the beginning of Beyond Love, Wyatt is twenty-one, with a good heart, but not enough experience in the world to understand the insidiousness of his father's manipulations.

It's only as he is pulled into the lies and deceit that he learns the true boundaries of his morals. Through the crucible of being tested time and again he learns the depth of his strength.

How many times have good people been taken advantage of by some unscrupulous someone? How many times has that person been their father?

Kara (Car-uh, not Care-uh) faces some of the same challenges. Her mother is smart, crazy, and suffers from Narcissistic Personality Disorder. (It's never diagnosed in the story, but it is the backbone of the character.) This is Kara's coming of age story, and as she grows, as she falls in love with Wyatt, she learns how all-encompassing her mother's presence is in her life and slowly extricates herself.

It's not easy, but I can't imagine that turning your back on a parent ever is.

In my opinion, quiet strength is the most powerful. It doesn't need the fireworks of spite and anger. It doesn't need harsh words, or the satisfaction of revenge. It simply is. A steel-infused spine and a heart clear of doubt...

Through their story Wyatt and Kara learn hard lessons about themselves, about their parents, about the nature and balance of strength. Their obstacles forge them into one heart, beating together.

And as the Hutton family learns everything these two struggled through over the years, they all take one giant step forward in healing from the havoc Burke wreaked on their hearts and minds.

Together.

PROLOGUE

WYATT

My family knew our father was the villain in our story. What they didn't know was he had an accomplice.

Me.

Wyatt Hutton. The optimist. The man with a quick laugh and easy smile. The hard-working second son who sacrificed his wants and needs for the greater good of his family.

While that might have been true in the beginning, by the time my father was done with me, it was only a façade. I didn't just keep his secrets, I helped him bury them. I lied. I cheated. I stole. Under his guidance, I explored the darkest sides of my personality, and as much as they disgusted me, I didn't turn away. Instead,

I embraced them, then covered it all up and put on a brave face for everyone else.

Burke Hutton—the patriarch of our family, publicly beloved for his philanthropy, privately loathed for his alcoholism—had a mistress. A mistress with a taste for the decadent. A mistress with a daughter.

The girl wasn't my father's child, though it might have been better if she was.

Maybe things wouldn't have gone so far.

Maybe my dad would have gotten tired of the woman if it wasn't for the girl—a child he seemed to love more than his own flesh and blood.

Maybe I wouldn't have made so many mistakes if it wasn't for her.

Kara Lockhart. Innocent. Off-limits. And in desperate need of my protection.

She and I existed on the razor's edge of hate and love.

She was the biggest secret—and deepest regret—of my life.

I

THEN

CHAPTER ONE

WYATT

Growing up, my dad's office was the most foreboding place in our home. Shrouded in shadows and stress, decorated with brooding masculinity and a firm, no-children policy, stepping over the threshold was akin to trespassing and punishable to the furthest extent of the law. As I aged and our home grew from a charming little bed and breakfast into a full-blown resort, I became a welcome asset in the room, but even now, as an adult, I found myself lingering in the doorway as if I needed permission to enter.

My father stood in front of the windows behind his desk, suitcoat draped over the back of his chair, shirtsleeves rolled up to his elbows. Seemingly unaware of my presence, he sipped whisky as he stared at the ocean behind the house. Sunlight sliced through the window, catching in his salt and pepper hair and hiding his face in shadow.

It seemed a fitting metaphor.

Darkness overtaking light.

The father he had been devoured by the drunk he had become.

Massive furniture dominated the room. An imposing desk—dark wood and hard angles, with a towering, black leather chair hunkering behind it. Giant bookshelves covered in tomes I doubted he even read loomed against the walls. Mom tried to soften the room by adding plants and flowers, as if the pops of color and life could chase away the dark, but it didn't help. The darkness always won.

"Jesus, Wyatt. In or out." Dad sipped his drink, never taking his eyes off the window, his posture dripping disdain. No matter what choice I made, it would be the wrong one. If I stepped into his office, I would be the worst interruption of his day. If I backed away, he would see me as weak and therefore not worth his time in the first place.

The urge to flip him the bird, walk out the front door, and keep on going until I was somewhere else

—*anywhere* else—was strong. It had been for years. But as always, the thought of leaving Mom, Eli, and Harlow to deal with Dad kept me stuck where I was. I chose to stay for them, positioning myself as a buffer between the members of my family. If I left, they would have to deal with the asshole my father had become, and they deserved better than that. And so, I pushed those darker thoughts away and focused on my many reasons to smile—health, wealth, and a (mostly) happy family.

As I stepped over the threshold, Dad turned. "Take a seat." He indicated the chair across from his desk, then lowered himself into his own with a scowl.

Burke Hutton became predatory when he hung out with Jack Daniels. His actions weren't accidentally cruel. They were purposefully malicious. Crafted with the sole intention of targeting a weakness—one he had personally installed—and striking with enough force to knock me off balance. Over the years, I had learned to read his posture, the curl of his lips, the glint in his eye. His demeanor as he regarded me over his desk warned me to brace myself.

"At twenty-one, you're almost enough of a man to see the world for what it is. Cruel and hard." The way he narrowed his eyes made me wonder if he knew he was also describing himself. "Not the fairy tale world your mother lives in," he added, almost under his breath.

Mom's consistent optimism had once been a trait my father admired. As the years passed and his drinking increased, he grew to look down on her ability to find the good in anything. He claimed it made her weak. Vulnerable and easily taken advantage of. I often wondered if his anger stemmed from some awareness that he was the one taking advantage. It had to be easier to point his hatred outward instead of looking inward.

Dad cleared his throat, claiming my attention. "It's time for me to bring you in on a bit of a family secret."

Though, as he launched into his story, it became clear this wasn't a family secret.

This was his secret.

And it was terrible.

I listened in shock as my father told me about the mistress he had been supporting for the last three years. A mistress with a daughter—not his, thank God —and expensive taste. When he noticed the rage boiling beneath my surface, he paused long enough to laugh, a sound that buried bitterness in the pit of my stomach.

"You go right ahead and look all high and mighty now," he said as clouds covered the sun, casting a shadow over the room, "but wait a few years. Marriage is a prison sentence and men—*real* men—are built for freedom." He threw back the rest of his drink and spun the glass on the desk. "I'm dying a slow death with your mother."

"You're dying a slow death because you drink too much." My mother was a beautiful woman with a generous heart, someone who went out of her way to help people. She was too good for my father, and everyone knew it—even him, though he would never admit it.

Burke's eyebrows hit his hairline and I braced myself for his spiteful retort. Instead, he smirked and poured himself another glass. "The sooner the better then, right?"

There was probably a part of all of us that felt that way, though we wouldn't admit it. There was something awful in knowing hatred filled a heart that should be brimming with love. Instead, we made plans to scatter to the wind as soon as we were able, severing the very ties that kept us strong when we were young.

My older brother Lucas had been so desperate to get away, he joined the Marines the day he graduated from high school. My younger brother Caleb moved out the day he turned eighteen, supporting himself on a part-time fast food salary as he finished his senior year.

Eli counted the days until he could do the same. And poor Harlow had basically disappeared into herself, drawing and writing and playing the guitar as if she thought she could find a way to exist entirely in her own head.

While I was lost in thought, Dad continued to drone on about the mistress and her daughter—Madeline and Kara. I hoped he would get to the point quickly so I could decide what I was going to do with this knowledge.

"Man...that Kara..." Dad zeroed in on me, his gaze sharp as he catalogued my reaction. "That girl is something else. Sixteen. Smart. Talented. Good at everything she does." Those exact words could be used to describe Harlow, but Dad treated her like he would be happier if she didn't exist. His lip curled as he went in for the kill. "You could learn a lot from her. She's got more balls than you'll ever have."

She also, apparently, had private school tuition that needed paying. A luxury dad's biological children never had because, in his opinion, we needed a good dose of reality that only public school could provide.

"Why are you telling me this?" I asked, though I assumed he needed to clear his conscience. Dragging me down with him was just icing on the cake. I was part priest, part co-conspirator—absolving him of his sins as he implicated me in his crimes.

"As I get older"—Dad paused to take another drink —"it's going to get harder for me to hide these things. Especially the financial stuff. Your mom's too smart for her own good."

When he said *older*, he meant *more of a drunk.* "And you want me to help you hide it." The realization was a bucket of ice water poured over my head. I wasn't built for lies or deceit. Those things planted worry in my stomach and the roots dug painfully through my bones. Love and trust were meant to be honored, not thrown to the side like trash in the gutter.

"My son, ladies and gentlemen." Dad hefted his glass. "A Mensa candidate for sure."

I let the barb roll off me like water. Showing Dad he hit a sensitive spot only gave him a place to aim the next time and I was getting pretty good at laughing off his insults. "I won't do this," I said. "I can't lie to Mom. To my brothers and sister. This is your mess. You deal with it."

The man across from me had once been everything a boy could hope for in a father. Loving and kind. Willing to build his dreams out of sweat and hard work, and competent in teaching his children to do the same. Somewhere along the way, the alcohol burned that man out of existence, leaving nothing but a shell of the person I once admired. The intelligence that had allowed him to build The Hutton Hotel out of nothing but my mother's hopes and dreams was now allocated to finding new ways to torture his family and further his addictions.

"You have to do this." Dad glared at me, all joviality falling from his face. "If this secret comes out, it will destroy us. The whole damn family will fall to pieces, and you know as well as anyone that the family is the reason the hotel is so successful. If we go to shit, so does the business, and then what will we have? Nothing. No money. No credibility. We'd lose the house. Lose each other. We'd be done. That's why I chose you. Caleb's too weak, Eli's too dumb, Lucas is gone, and Harlow's head is filled with fluff. But you... you always do what's right." Dad lifted his glass. "Even when it's stupid."

An hour later, we pulled to a stop in front of a pretentious condo with manicured lawns, drooping palms, and a price tag so high, it made my head spin.

"What does Madeline do for a living?" I asked as I shut the car door behind me, swallowing a groan as the heat and humidity of the Florida Keys in July stole my breath. Saying her name felt dirty, like I was making room for her in my head and I really didn't want her there.

"Me." Dad smirked over his shoulder as he strode up the walk.

Great. So the mistress had expensive taste and no way to support it without dipping into my father's wallet. I took in the soaring architecture and pristine landscaping, trying to figure out the monthly rent, imagining dollar signs on everything I saw. "Let me guess. You pay for all of this."

The front door burst open as a bleached-blonde tornado siren came screeching into Dad's arms. "Burkey!" she squealed, her bright red lips cracking into a crocodile smile.

Dad grabbed the woman's breast and gave it a squeeze. "Paid for these, too," he said to me, while Madeline laughed and swatted at his hand. He flashed me a grin like a slap in the face.

Over the years, I thought I had come to terms with the man my father had become. That while he wasn't perfect, we'd all found a sense of equilibrium, making the best out of a bad thing. But standing on that sidewalk, watching him grope a woman who was not my mother, I realized there was nothing left of the man he used to be—of the man I secretly wished he would still be.

Madeline required an introduction, clearly unaware that Burke Hutton had kids. "Your son, huh?" She leered at me as thoughts ticked away behind cruel eyes. "It sure is a pleasure to get to know you," she purred, before calling over her shoulder, "Kara! Baby! Come here! There's someone you just have to meet!"

The last person I wanted to meet was the girl. I hadn't wanted to meet the mother, but that seemed a necessary evil as I would now be directly involved with helping her maintain her lifestyle. Meeting the girl—a child who made my father smile when I couldn't remember the last time any of his real family had managed that particular feat—felt like a step too far.

And the grin on Dad's face told me he agreed. Why did he take such pleasure in my discomfort? And for that matter, why did I care? He was a bitter old man intent on self-destruction. Instead of letting him drag me down, I focused on a drooping palm swaying in the breeze and the unending stretch of sky behind it until something, this sense of urgency, this *knowing*, demanded my attention.

Hey, the something whispered. *Look up. This is important. Look up. Now.*

"Well if it isn't Daddy Warbucks." Her voice wrapped around me like smoke, unusually deep for a female, almost rusty, and sexy as hell. It sent chills down my spine, and despite my best efforts to keep my gaze on the ground, I met her eyes.

She was young. Too young. Dark hair hung over delicate shoulders. Heart-shaped lips sat in a small face with large, gray eyes. Eyes that narrowed when they landed on mine.

"Wyatt Hutton," she murmured, half-prayer. Half-curse.

"Well, how did you know that when I didn't even know Burkey had kids?" Madeline squawked.

The glance the girl threw her mother's way was filled with enough disdain that even I caught it. "Because he talks about his kids sometimes? You never listen to anyone, do you?"

Burke pulled Kara in for a hug and my heart broke for my little sister. Harlow craved our father's approval like an addict craved her next fix, and here this Kara had him wrapped around her little finger. As Dad pressed a kiss into her hair, I caught a glimpse of the man he used to be. A man we all mourned, even though we still saw him every day.

In that moment, I hated Kara Lockhart. I hated her on behalf of my brothers and sister. I hated her on behalf of my mother. I hated her because my dad was right. If any of this got out, it would rip our family to pieces. I hated her because I knew I would keep his secret. And with that thought in my head, I realized I hated myself a little, too.

"Wyatt," Dad said when he released her, "meet Kara Lockhart. The daughter I should have had."

The more I knew about these people, the deeper I

would be pulled into Dad's secrets and lies, so I offered the girl a curt nod instead of a greeting and gave my attention to back to my feet.

CHAPTER TWO

Kara

Wyatt Hutton wouldn't look at me. Which was fine because when he did, it was like I was a piece of gum stuck to the bottom of his shoe. Like he couldn't believe he had to stand so close to a piece of trash like me.

Like I wasn't worth his time.

A flare of anger demanded I march right up to him and prove I didn't belong in the same box as my mother. The fact that he put me there without so much as a hello told me everything I needed to know about him.

He wasn't worth *my* time.

He was, however, much hotter in person than he was on Facebook. One of those people who didn't photograph well because his beauty was the kind that moved. I'd heard that line in a song once and never understood it until seeing Wyatt. But now, it made a magical kind of sense. Looking at him made me feel hopeful, which in turn made me feel ridiculous because it was clear he didn't like me.

He was tall—taller than I thought he would be. The resemblance to his dad was obvious, but also not immediately clear. Burke was like a redwood. Strong and sturdy. Thick arms, thick body, and thick legs. His personality took up massive amounts of space. Wyatt, on the other hand, was long-limbed. He had broad shoulders and a tapered waist. He was blonde where Burke was dark and smiled while Burke scowled. They were opposite sides of the coin, these men, though I wasn't sure what to do with that thought.

The most stunning thing about Wyatt was his eyes —even if I only saw them for a second before he refused to look at me again. They were such a light blue, they seemed to shine with a light of their own. For the heartbeat of time he deigned to favor me with his attention, they stole my breath.

I thought I would hate him. I thought I'd hate all of the Hutton kids, really. After all, they were living the life I would never have. They had two parents with stable jobs. They lived in a beautiful house that wasn't paid for with someone else's money. They were local royalty. Everyone knew the Hutton name, and no one had a bad thing to say about them.

The moment I looked at Wyatt, I realized I couldn't hate him—though it was obvious the feeling wasn't mutual. For as much as I thought he had the life I wanted, I had something of his, something he desperately craved.

His dad.

The image of the Huttons I had built by stalking their Facebook accounts was false. Their life was nowhere near the golden Utopia I daydreamed about. And how dumb did I have to be to ever think it was? I knew Burke was a cheat. I knew he was a drunk, too.

I guess I assumed that because he was so good to me, he was that good to everyone. That his own children knew him the way I did. Just five minutes of watching the way Burke treated his son blasted that idea out of the water. In fact, for a moment, I had an uncomfortable sense of kinship with Wyatt. He was a pawn for his father the same way I was a pawn for my mother. At best, we were tools they could use to further their own selfish endeavors. At worst...

...well, sometimes it was better not to think about the worst.

The days Mom couldn't drag herself out of bed and three-year-old me was left to figure out breakfast for herself. The oversharing of information, things no daughter should learn about her mother, as if we were best friends instead of flesh and blood.

As awkward as those days were, I much preferred them to the days where she had nothing but contempt for my existence. The days when simply seeing my face or hearing me move in my room brought her rage boiling to the surface. I spent so many years wondering what I'd done to make her hate me so much, but only recently realized that I hadn't done anything but take her attention away from the thing she valued most: herself. She resented me for the heinous act of being born. For weighing her down with responsibility and adding stretch marks to her belly and breasts. As if I had any say in the matter.

I had the uncomfortable realization that, in Wyatt's eyes, I wasn't all that much different from my mother. She was the other woman and I was the other child, both of us selfish enough to take time and attention from a man who wouldn't give it to his family.

And while I couldn't muster hate for Wyatt, I felt a heavy dose of resentment toward him. It wasn't like I chose this. It wasn't like I told my mom to sleep with a married man, then suck him dry for every spare dollar he would throw her way. I didn't ask for the fancy condo. Or the expensive car. It wasn't me who begged for the private school tuition, though I knew enough to value the education I was getting—it would be the key that set me free from this life.

I didn't ask to be born to a woman who was willing to sell her body to get what she wanted. I didn't ask to grow up without a father, without even an inkling as to who he was or what he looked like. I didn't ask to be my mother's keeper. And I certainly didn't ask for the way she kept looking from me to Wyatt and back again. She was hatching a plot with me at the center. I could see it in her eyes and whatever it was, I was sure to hate it.

I only had to survive this life for two more years and I would be free. Two more years until my eighteenth birthday, and I was out of here. I didn't have a clue where I would go, but at least I had the balls to look at my situation and know I had to get out. Wyatt couldn't even do that. He was five years older and still stuck at home, kowtowing to a man he obviously couldn't stand.

The little ball of hate I'd been building sputtered back to life. I glanced up, ready to eviscerate him with a single look, and my heart fluttered in protest when he met my gaze.

Despite myself, I smiled, which made him smile in return. It was a beautiful thing, warm and genuine and damn if hope didn't come rushing back to life, filling me with a sense of...of...the thought was gone before it could fully form. Wyatt looked away, rubbing a hand over his mouth and looking worried, and all the dark thoughts from before rushed back in to cover up that brief moment of light.

Confused, I said my goodbyes to Burke and retreated to the safety of my room.

CHAPTER THREE

WYATT

Days passed and my father's secret spun like poison in my gut. I couldn't look at my mom. Or my brothers. Or my sister. I could barely look at myself and I definitely couldn't stand to be around Dad. The urge to tuck myself away in my room and never come out was strong, but isolation wasn't in my nature. Instead, I threw myself into my work, helping guests, learning the books, and finding new and inventive ways to hide my dad's misdeeds.

A lesser man would have driven himself to drink. Thankfully, while I wasn't a great man, I was strong enough to resist. I learned to exist on two levels—the happy, optimistic version of myself I presented to the world. The version I knew I could be all the time if only...

...if only...

Beneath that layer coursed a river of anxiety. A litany of repressed anger and frustration caused by the minutia of everyday life. I could never relax and be myself, lest that river make its way to the surface and surprise everyone with the strength of its currents. I wanted to be the light in everyone else's day, and that meant I had to swallow the darkness. I feared it was eating me from the inside out.

As time marched on and my world didn't come crashing down, life settled into something resembling normal. My mother didn't accuse me of treachery. My father almost treated me like a human being instead of a fleck of lint on his favorite suit.

I devoted myself to making my family feel good, and through that, I found a sense of purpose. I joked them into laughter when they were feeling down. I helped my brother and sister with homework or school drama. In my mind, I became a sort of umbrella, protecting them from the difficulties of life and as days passed, I started to believe everything was going to be alright. Life had its ups and downs. Sure, things felt bad now, but that only meant it would make the good times feel so much sweeter when we got there.

It was only at night, when I was alone, that things

got hard. As I lay in bed, staring at the ceiling and wishing for sleep, the weight of my father's secret settled on my chest, so heavy I could barely breathe. My heart would pound and my stomach would churn and my mind would present a parade of questions and hypothetical situations for me to consider.

What if I told Mom? Would the family dissolve the way Dad said it would? Or would it finally relieve her of having to deal with the monster her husband had become? She could walk away with her head held high and her dignity intact...or maybe she would tell me she was disappointed to learn I was just like him.

What if I told Lucas? He was far enough away, busy being a big bad Marine, that maybe it wouldn't affect him. Maybe he would have some advice...or maybe he would call me an asshole and never speak to me again.

What if I told Dad to shove his secret up his ass?

What if I confronted Madeline?

...what if...

...what if...

...what if...?

Night after night, I wrestled my demons, my father's threats of disaster battling my need to be honest and upfront. In this case, the truth felt like a weapon. One I'd been given to hold and one I chose to keep sheathed. I decided to bear the weight alone, so my mother didn't have to. And as days bled into weeks, the choice felt more and more like the right one.

I was a good person doing a bad thing.

At least that was what I told myself.

With thoughts like that drumming around my brain, I headed to Caleb's apartment to help him build his new entertainment system. At nineteen, my younger brother was striving for self-sufficiency, recently becoming manager at the fast food restaurant he had worked at since he was old enough to get a job.

He took the position because he needed the money, but immediately began looking for better ways to earn a living. Caleb said the promotion was a wakeup call. He knew he had more to give than a life flipping burgers, even if he didn't know what that looked like yet. In the meantime, he used the increase in salary to buy some much needed furnishings for the apartment he shared with Derek, a sleaze-ball whose main focus in life was seeing how wasted he could get and how many girls he could bring home.

Caleb answered my knock on his door with a scowl, then shuffled out of the way without so much as a word. His hair stood on end. Pillow marks were etched into his cheek. His puffy eyes struggled to focus. My brother had never woken up easily and I could see the remnants of the little kid he used to be in the set of his shoulders. As an adult, he was the biggest of us

Hutton kids, which was ironic because he spent his childhood scrawny.

"Good morning to you, sunshine," I said as I stepped into the nearly empty apartment.

Caleb ran a hand along the back of his neck and grumbled something that could have been a greeting. Or, he just cursed my name. With him, it was hard to tell.

"Looks like Captain Dickhead struck again." I gestured toward Derek's closed door and the stream of women's clothing leading right to it. A scrap of fabric that might have been a skirt. A bit of lace. A sequined top.

"Sure did." Caleb ran his hands into his hair, causing it to stick up even worse than it already was. "All night long. Banging some chick who wouldn't stop screeching the loudest, fakest orgasm of all time." He ambled into the kitchen. "Coffee?"

"Sounds great," I said, as he grabbed two mugs out of the cabinet. "I know I've said it, but congrats again on that promotion. I'm really proud of you."

Caleb scoffed as he poured his coffee. "Just living up to my full potential here." His self-deprecating tone wasn't lost on me and I immediately set about trying to make him feel better. Sure, he didn't intend to finish his life in fast food, but it would do him some good to slow down and see the accomplishment for what it was—a good thing and a great way to jumpstart his life.

"I don't know, Moose," I said, smiling wide. "Management at nineteen seems like a big deal to me."

The compliment made him obviously uncomfortable, but he offered me a smile anyway. "Thanks, man." He blew over the rim of his mug, his eyes a million miles away. When they settled on mine, what I saw in them made me nervous.

"Hey, Wy? I need to talk to you about something," Caleb began.

My heart jumped into my throat because holy shit, he knew. Somehow, he found out what I was doing for Dad and I was finally going to have to face the truth. As much as I knew I'd earned what was coming, that didn't stop me from dreading it.

Caleb cleared his throat and dropped his gaze to the ground. "I've been thinking, maybe I can save up enough money to buy a boat. Move down to Key West and start a business. Take tourists out for snorkeling or some shit like that. I'd be in charge of my own future, and on the water all day instead of coming home smelling like burger grease. Maybe, you know, I could even live on the boat for a while to save money. Or something." Uncertainty clung to his words.

Relief surged through me, followed closely by regret and a heavy dash of guilt. My brother wasn't looking to confront me. He wanted my advice. Because I was Wyatt, the dependable older brother. The carbon copy of our optimistic mother. The Hutton you could trust to support you and brainstorm ways to turn bad ideas into good ones.

Reminding myself to calm down and breathe more, I leaned against the wall, grinning at Caleb, proud of him for looking for better ways to live. He would be happy on the water all day and had a quiet charisma the tourists would appreciate.

"You know you could do that at The Hut," I said, referring to our family business—The Hutton Hotel. "Wouldn't even have to come up with the money for a boat because the hotel already has one. And you could just move back into your old room, so you wouldn't have to worry about rent. Every dollar you made could go directly to saving up a nest egg. You know Mom would be thrilled to have you back. And the pay would be good. Better than if you opened your own business for sure."

Caleb shook his head the entire time I spoke, rejecting the idea from the moment he knew what I was saying. "Not gonna happen. Dad never did a damn thing for us. As long as he's around, I have every intention of returning that favor. He's on his own." He glanced at me and shrugged an apology, then glared at the wall.

His words dredged up a memory of Caleb in elementary school. He was always tall, but back then, his energy went into growing up, not out. He was long and lanky. Thin and easily offended. He'd been a target for the other boys, at least until he hit puberty and filled out. When things were at their worst, Mom brought up private school, or even homeschool as an option, but Dad had snapped at her to stop coddling him.

The boy has to learn how to grow thicker skin, he said as Mom fussed over Caleb's swelling lip, a gift from a particularly persistent asshole kid overdue for a fat lip of his own.

An image of Kara Lockhart slithered through my mind, with her sullen voice and private school tuition. That had been happening since the day we met. Out of nowhere, I would find myself thinking of her—which was a waste of energy because she only made me mad. I didn't like her, and the feeling had obviously been mutual, though I couldn't figure out why. She had everything I always wanted. My father's love. His respect. His guidance. Yet, she also had the nerve to look at me like I was the asshole in the situation.

I tried to brush her off as young and immature. It was natural for her to see the situation that way because teenagers were little narcissists who always saw the world in terms of themselves. But I couldn't let her off the hook that easily. Two of my brothers and my sister were still teenagers and I could guaran-damn-tee that if they were in Kara's situation, they would be mature enough to realize the money paying for that private school tuition was coming from a man who had children of his own to take care.

Children of his own he *wasn't* taking care of.

Caleb and I resorted to silence while we built his entertainment system. Thinking about Kara had ruined my mood and Caleb was never much of a talker in the first place. As we worked and the silence between us stretched longer, my anger sent little sparks of indignation out toward Kara. I wanted to talk to Caleb about it. I wanted to explain what I'd learned and to ask his advice.

But I couldn't. For one, he was younger than me and was in no way prepared to offer advice on something so complicated. And for two, Caleb already lived in a constant state of anger when it came to Dad. If I told him what I knew, his rage would burn hot and bright until it devoured him. Nothing would be left of his gentle soul. He would go to Dad, ready to combust, and the aftershocks of his rage would shake the family to pieces.

After we finished the work, I gave my brother a thump on the back and left before I could change my mind about telling him. I drove with no clue as to where I was going, just a tornado of destructive thoughts whipping my emotions into a frenzy. For as many times as I tried to bring things back to my father, or to Madeline, my brain kept circling back to Kara.

Intellectually, I knew she was caught up in the mistakes of her parent—just like me. But I wasn't in the mood for rational thought. I was in the mood to point fingers and lay blame. I was in the mood to self-destruct.

I pulled to a stop at a red light and frowned at the building in front of me. On some level, I had to have known where I was going. I had to have been perfectly aware I chose to drive to this particular spot. As much as I wanted to claim it was an accident for me to end up in front of Kara's fancy, private school, I knew it wasn't. It couldn't be. Not with the way she had spun through my thoughts since the day her mother presented her to me like some fancy prize she knew I would claim.

After a month of staring at the school address on the invoices, I finally caved. I wanted to see what she had that my brother and sister didn't. It was no accident that I was where I was. It was, however, an accident that I arrived exactly as school let out.

Streams of students poured across the road in front of me, barely pausing to make sure traffic had stopped, safe in their assumption of immortality. They laughed with friends, backpacks bouncing, books clutched to chests, and jokes flung over the crowd with an air of confidence reserved for the young.

Two girls paused on the walk, catching my attention. Though the plaid skirts and white shirts they wore were identical, they couldn't have been more different. One was tall and thin, blonde and vibrant. The other was small and curvy, with dark hair, olive skin, and gray eyes that hardened when they met mine.

One was a stranger. A normal teenager doing normal, teenaged things.

The other was Kara Lockhart.

She glared at me, catching the attention of her friend who followed her gaze to land on mine. I knew what it looked like. A man my age, parked in front of her school, staring her down as she crossed the street.

I expected fear to tighten Kara's features.

I expected her to misunderstand.

I expected her to freak out.

I certainly didn't expect her to arch an eyebrow, flip me the bird, and walk away without another glance.

CHAPTER FOUR

KARA

My mother, ladies and gentlemen. A pillar of parental responsibility. Capable of seeing her teenaged daughter in danger and leaping into inspired action. Taking out bad guys in one ferocious swipe of her mama-bear rage.

Oh, wait.

No.

Never mind.

My mom was the one who learned some creep was stalking her daughter outside school and decided to play matchmaker.

"Mom!" I held out my hands in exasperation because even though I knew it was worthless to argue, I couldn't *not* try to get her to see the situation for what it was. Wrong! "He was parked right there. Just glaring out his window at me. There was malice in his eyes, Mom. *Malice.*" I popped my hand on my hip. "I don't feel safe."

"Oh, Kara. You are too dramatic, you silly little thing!" Mom swiped a dress—a skin-tight red number with a low front and an embarrassingly short skirt—out of her closet and held it against her body, meeting my gaze through the floor length mirror. "I knew Wyatt was interested in you. I could just feel it. Oh, baby. This is such a good thing!"

I plopped on Mom's bed, remembering the intensity in Wyatt's stare as he watched Brooke and me cross the street. As an early bloomer, I was all too aware what boys looked like when they were interested. Wyatt Hutton did not look at me like that. "Interested in me? You mean intent on planning my abduction and subsequent murder. Where exactly is this good thing you're talking about?"

"Wyatt isn't a kidnapper," Mom murmured, her attention still mostly on her reflection.

"Right. Because you know him so well? You didn't even know Burke had kids."

Mom whirled. "Well, no. But anyone could see that man is gentle and kind." She grinned like she was already planning our double wedding—mother and daughter to father and son. "You guys would be so good together."

"What? Mom! Ew!"

"I'm just saying, Burkey's fortune is going to have to go to someone when he dies." She leveled me with a look that meant she expected me to fill in the blanks for myself. Which I did. Easily. Her thoughts typically spiraled around finding a man, getting her claws in him, and siphoning away his money. But there was no way I would give her the satisfaction of hearing me say something so despicable.

When she got tired of my silence, Mom gave me a little verbal nudge. "And given how much Burkey loves you, wouldn't it just be peachy if his money could go to you?" And, by her logic, if I was dating his son, that would be a surefire way to seal the deal.

She and I sparred like this all the time. She tried to lead me right up to a bad idea, set it up so I was the one to actually speak the words, and then when things exploded, she could blame it all on me. After a life-time of living that way, I caught on last year, then spent a solid week looking back at all the 'mistakes' of my life, wondering if my mom was a moron or master-mind. Had she intentionally made me feel like every-thing I touched fell to pieces? Or was she just a disaster of a human being who had stellar instincts when it came to keeping herself free of blame? I spent more time contemplating that question than I wanted to admit.

"Does it not bother you that Wyatt is five years older than me? That I am still a child and he is an adult, legally able to drink and vote and own a firearm?"

"Believe me, Poopsie," Mom replied, trotting out the nickname she knew I despised. "With a body like the one you're rocking, you do not count as a child. Besides, five years isn't that big of a difference. When you're twenty-one, he'll be twenty-six. What's the big deal?"

"But I'm not twenty-one. I'm sixteen. And so, you know, that right there is the big deal."

Mom rolled her eyes. "It's only a big deal if you make it a big deal."

How could this woman be even remotely related to me? How could she look at her completely inexperienced daughter, *me*, the girl who hadn't even had a serious boyfriend yet—a choice I made to avoid becoming like her—and be totally cool with her dating a full-blown man?

A man who just happened to be the son of her boyfriend?

A man who had been busy stalking children outside their school that very day?

The truth was, the glimpses I got of Wyatt by

following his social media lined up with Mom's assessment: Wyatt wasn't a kidnapper. I had never seen a picture of him without a giant, friendly smile in place. Or heard a story where he wasn't hard-working, or charitable, or involved in something amazing.

Though, if you looked at the stuff Burke polished up and showed to the social media world, you could say the same about him. On the outside, he looked like a real gem. It was only when you got to know him that you realized he wasn't as perfect as he pretended to be. It made me wonder what secrets his son could be hiding.

"Well, listen," I said, standing up and putting on my toughest face. "When you see Burke tonight, please tell him to call off his dog."

Mom pulled another dress—tighter and shorter and redder than the last—out of her closet and held it up for comparison. "I'm not seeing Burke tonight." She gave me a hard look through the mirror before conjuring up a sweet smile. "You'll be on your own for dinner, though. And I won't be home until late. Like so late it'll be early, if you know what I mean. Maybe you should invite Brooke over to spend the night?"

I broke eye contact, wondering if I would ever be comfortable with how open she was about her sex life. "It's a school night."

"So? Don't stay up too late. Or do! You only live once, you know?"

Part of me resented the fact that she cheated on Burke. The part that appreciated he paid for our rent, our car, and my school. The part that recognized how kind he was to me. The part that wondered if he was misunderstood by his own wife and kids. I felt sorry for him because my mother was a parasite. Her survival was dependent on deriving the money and attention she needed at anyone else's expense.

But the rest of me knew that Karma was a bitch. Burke was a cheater dating a whore. There was no illusion of love or comfort between them. He used her for sex and she used him for money and somehow, they were fine with the state of things between them.

While Mom finished getting ready for her date with Backup Guy—she liked to have someone waiting in the wings in case Burke ditched her and we found ourselves homeless—I stormed into my room and pulled up my newest fixation: Wyatt Hutton's Facebook account.

His posts had changed tone recently. They weren't as frequent. And as much as his pictures still had his trademark smile, his eyes looked strained. Maybe that was because he was busy plotting the abduction and murder of a certain teenaged girl. A teenaged girl whose mother just left for the night without so much as a goodbye or twenty-dollar bill with which to figure out dinner.

Lucky for me, I had been saving for my grand escape since I was twelve, squirreling away birthday money like my life depended on it. Over the years, I had accumulated quite a sizeable sum in an old shoebox I tucked into the back of my closet and covered with blankets. After I got a part-time job earlier this year, Mom had been adamant about setting up a savings account for me, and as the custodian of the account, she had full access to everything. I put just over half of each paycheck in there and pretended not to notice when she helped herself. Every other dollar I earned was stashed in that shoebox. If she knew how much money I had, well, I wouldn't have it anymore. And there was no way I'd be able to leave the Keys at eighteen if I didn't have money.

I swiped a couple bills out of my stash and sent a text to Brooke, letting her know I was heading to Bricks & Mortar—a wannabe posh pizza parlor—and humbly requested her company. Without waiting for a reply, I locked up and hopped on my bicycle. The wind stirred up by movement felt good as my hair fluttered behind me, and the energy I spent pumping my legs helped to burn through the frustration I always felt after dealing with Mom.

"Jesus." Brooke rolled her eyes as I pulled to a stop

in front of her brand-new Volkswagen Beetle. "Really? Still with the bike?" She pushed out of the car in a flounce of blonde curls and energy.

"Yes. Still with the bike. Some of us don't have rich daddies to keep us in top of the line automobiles and an unending supply of gasoline with which to further destroy the environment."

Brooke blew out a puff of air. "I'm sure, somewhere, there's someone with more than enough money to buy you a car. Your mom just hasn't found him yet."

I hit her with a hard look, refusing to grace that statement with a response.

Brooke laughed, a breezy sound. "What? Too far? Was that a boundary?" As the only non-Lockhart person in existence who knew my story, she knew very well there were no boundaries between us.

I threw an arm around her shoulder. "Definitely too far. I'll never speak to you again. Now, tell me all about your day."

Laughing, we sauntered through the front door and Brooke paused. "Oh!" She turned to me, waving away the hostess with a hold-on-a-sec gesture. "There's a party this weekend. At Ryan Smeltzer's house. His parents are gone, so, you know what that means."

"A torrid night of debauchery and bad decisions?" I asked, fully aware of what happened to my friend when she got anywhere near a party.

"Exactly. And what's a night filled with bad decisions without you to save me when I make too many?" Brooke asked before relenting to the hostess and following her to a booth in the middle of the restaurant.

"I don't know." I pretended to be trying to make up my mind. "Don't you think you'd be too embarrassed of me if I showed up on my bike? I'd hate for you to have to find a way to live that down."

"That's why I'll pick you up!" Brooke smiled. "Come on, Todd Hudgins will be there!" She sing-songed the last bit, certain it would be the nail in the coffin.

And, as usual, she was right.

CHAPTER FIVE

WYATT

I always loved the dining room in The Hut. The giant table, big enough to fit all seven of us, made from strong and sturdy wood. To me, it represented the strength of our family and was the source of a wealth of memories.

When I was younger, Mom always took the time to cook a full meal on the weeknights and a giant brunch every Saturday. Back then, Dad used to help. He would pull her into his arms and press kisses into the top of her head, swaying to some song only the two of them could hear. We would take our places at the table, excitedly talking about our days around mouthfuls of food. We'd dream about the future. What The Hut might become. What *we* might become.

In my memories, the sun always shone, spilling through the giant picture windows like fairy dust on a perfect scene. No one ever got mad. Feelings never got hurt. And Dad never drank.

Life didn't look like that anymore, though I did my best to recreate it for my siblings. By the time Eli, Caleb, and Harlow were old enough to join us for dinner, Dad was drunk more than he was sober, so I did what I could to take his place, smiling when he frowned, encouraging when he scoffed at childish achievements.

Today, I walked into the dining room to find Eli at the table, blankly staring at a slew of books and papers spread out in front of him. I pulled out a heavy chair and plopped down. "Uhhh...what exactly is going on here?" I asked, feigning confusion.

He stared at me, good humor glinting in his eyes. "It's what they call homework, Wy. You know, a specific torture device designed by the old and bitter to inflict pain on those of us who are still young and beautiful." He ran his hands through his thick hair, once blonde like the rest of us, but getting darker each year.

"I know what it is, jackass," I replied with a laugh. "I just don't think I've ever seen you doing it before. Hence my confusion."

"Maybe I'm feeling inspired." Eli gave me a

lopsided grin. Both of us knew all too well that nothing about school inspired him. Ever.

"Or," Mom said, as she swooped into the room, pausing to ruffle her youngest son's hair, "maybe he's been told he won't be going to Homecoming if he doesn't get his grades up."

Eli ducked out of her grasp. "Or that."

I peered at the papers in front of him. "Now that sounds so much more like the Eli I know and love." School might not have been an inspiration to my youngest brother, but girls and parties? Those were things he could appreciate. Eli sat back, his attention on the waves on the other side of the window, whatever effort he had been willing to give his homework dwindling by the second.

Mom pulled out a chair and sat, her attention following Eli's. "Have either of you seen Harlow?"

"It's ten in the morning on a Saturday," I replied. "My guess is she's still in bed."

Mom shook her head. "First place I checked."

"What about down by the dock?" That was Harlow's happy place. When things were perfect, she would sit and let her feet dangle over the edge and stare at the water. She swore her inspiration whispered to her from beneath the waves.

"Second place I checked." Mom grimaced, which made me grimace, too.

If Harlow wasn't in her happy place, that meant it was a bad day and we might not find her for hours. And when we did, she would be lost in her thoughts and almost totally unreachable. I was in the middle of wondering what might have happened this early on a weekend to deem it a bad day, when a shadow loomed in the doorway, presenting me with the answer.

"Wyatt." Dad barked my name like an order and without another word, turned on his heel and stalked toward the office.

Eli scowled after him. "Have you ever considered not following him?" he asked. "Just let him sit in there and rot?"

"Plenty of times," I replied, staring at the now empty doorway.

"Why haven't you?"

Because if I did, Dad would take his anger out on Eli. And Mom. And Harlow. Because I was strong enough to take his shit and not let it affect me, but would hate myself if, for one minute, his wrath fell on anyone else.

I shrugged and ruffled Eli's hair. "Good luck with the homework," I said before walking out the door. My brother thought I was weak. That was fine. He could think whatever he wanted because I knew it wasn't true.

When I walked into the office, I found Dad perched on the edge of his desk, a glass of whisky in his hand. Because obviously, that was what every man needed at ten in the morning on a Saturday.

"I need you to run an errand for me."

"You realize if you held off on the drinking, you could run your errands yourself."

Dad lifted an eyebrow but didn't pounce. Instead, he crossed the room and wrapped an arm around my shoulder, drawing me in close to whisper as he led me deeper into the office. "Kara's in jail."

I knew that girl was trouble the moment I saw her. The feeling had crept through the air between us, an undeniable *something*. I couldn't name it, but I could tell she was going to wreak havoc on my life for as long as she was part of it. "Of course she is."

"Don't be like that. Kara is a good girl."

I rolled my eyes. "Oh, right. Silly me. There I go getting confused again. I mean, they always put the good girls in jail. What am I thinking?"

"I'm telling you." Dad pulled me even tighter, his arm a vice around my upper back. "Don't be like that."

I lifted his arm off my shoulder and stepped aside. "And I'm telling you, maybe you should worry about your own daughter before you go off rescuing someone else's."

Dad stiffened. "Harlow is wasting herself on all that writing and music nonsense. Kara, on the other hand, is gonna be something."

Kara, also, had spent the entire night in jail on drug charges. Her mother couldn't bail her out because she was drunk and had called Dad for help this morning. He, also drunk, couldn't collect the juvenile delinquent because he had appearances to keep up. And so, the burden fell to me.

Wyatt, the good guy.

The co-conspirator.

The man you went to when your mistress' daughter needed bail.

With anyone else, I would have made a joke, but my sense of humor was lost on Dad. Instead, I got the information I needed and headed downtown, humming the theme to the TV show *Cops*.

Kara

If Wyatt was cold the day we met, he was downright arctic as he collected me from jail. With barely more than a *hello* spoken between us, he filled out some paperwork, paid an undisclosed amount of money, and then stormed out of the building, expecting me to trail after him like a lost puppy.

Which I did. At first. But then pride got the better of me. He had obviously decided I was guilty without asking me what happened. While yes, things looked bad—he was picking me up from jail after all—I deserved a chance to explain. To show my displeasure, I purposefully went as slow as I could on my way to the parking lot, pausing more than once to enjoy the sweet smell of fresh air. By the time I lowered myself into the passenger seat of his car, Wyatt's jaw pulsed with anger.

"I didn't do it, by the way," I said as I strapped myself in.

Nothing.

"But, you know, thanks for judging me without knowing the whole story."

"I know enough," he bit out through a clenched jaw.

"But do you?" I asked, arching an eyebrow. "Do you really?"

With his attention firmly focused on the road in front of him, Wyatt replied, "I know you are sixteen years old and have just spent your first night in jail."

"How do you know it was my first night?"

That got his attention. Score one for Kara.

Wyatt turned to me with wide eyes and I couldn't help but laugh at his shocked expression. "Looks like you don't have everything figured out after all, big guy."

"That makes two of us," he muttered, before he gave his attention back to the road without another word.

"It was," I said a few minutes later, the silence getting the better of me. When Wyatt didn't reply, I clarified. "My first time in jail."

And I only had to spend the night because my mother was too drunk to come get me. Figures. I was the one in trouble for drugs, and she was the one too inebriated to come to my rescue. Instead, my knight in shining armor was an asshole in a pair of shorts and a T-shirt.

Wyatt gave me a look I couldn't decipher, kindness softening his pale blue eyes even as his lips pulled into a frown. "Congratulations."

"Ahh. He speaks." I knew it would be better for me to shut up and accept the ride home with grace. I just couldn't help myself. The moment he decided to judge me was the moment I decided to make his life a living hell. Brooke told me I had a warrior's spirit. I tried to see it as a compliment, but part of me realized that being ready to butt heads at a moment's notice was a weakness of mine.

Wyatt turned to me, still trying to look mad, but I didn't think his face was designed for it. "Believe me," he said. "You really don't want to hear what I have to say."

"Really? Try me." I folded my arms over my chest and lifted my eyebrows. Anything was better than the stony silence he seemed set on delivering.

"Okay, fine. I think you are a self-entitled child who is too comfortable spending my father's money and stupid enough to waste her life on drugs. Happy now?" he asked, then gave his attention back to the road.

"I already told you I didn't do it. Hence, the whole me coming home thing. I don't think they let the guilty ones go home."

Turned out, the house party got a little out of control. Okay, a lot out of control. College kids showed up, some of them with pot and other such illicit substances. Brooke got wasted with Ryan Smeltzer and I found a quiet place to be until I could figure out how to get myself home. Turned out, once the cops were called, the kids with the drugs were smart enough to get the hell out of Dodge and Ryan Smeltzer was more than willing to point a finger at me. Brooke, as usual, was too wasted to be of much help. Tada! Kara Lock-hart now had a criminal record.

Fat lot of good it would do me to explain the story to Captain Asshole over there. Bored, I stared out the window, stifling yawns and composing self-righteous speeches while Wyatt navigated the streets. As he pulled to a stop in front of the condo, I grabbed the door handle, ready to yank it open and put as much space between us as absolutely possible.

Wyatt caught my wrist, stopping me. "Look," he said, his voice gruff. "Whether or not you did it isn't the issue."

"Oh yeah?" I stared down at his hand around my wrist, ignoring the lightning strikes of adrenaline brought on by his touch. I didn't know what they meant, but I liked the way it felt and that couldn't be good. "Pray tell. What exactly is the issue?"

"The problem is that you are sixteen years old and putting yourself in the kind of situations that end up with you in jail," Wyatt replied, his frustration rising as I forced him to explain what he obviously thought I should already understand.

"And?"

"And you should stop."

I yanked out of his grasp. "Right. Noted. Thanks for the ride," I bit off as I pushed open the door. "I'm perfectly capable of taking care of myself, by the way." Growing up with Madeline Lockhart had been Independence Bootcamp and I graduated with honors.

Wyatt rolled his eyes. "Looks like it."

I stared for a few exasperated seconds, then slammed the door in his face. The asshole didn't even flinch. He just yanked the car in gear and drove away without looking back.

Wyatt

Kara had tried so hard to look strong. Or brave. Or some combination of the two. All I saw was a little girl who needed help and didn't have anyone to lean on. I couldn't imagine her mom set much of an example, other than how to make married men cheat on their wives or how to be too drunk to rescue the people who depended on you.

I kept imagining Harlow in that situation and gave Kara the same speech I would have given her. As important as it was to have people in your life to protect you, the sooner you could do it for yourself, the better. Of course, Kara's pride kept her from hearing what I was trying to say. Instead of a thoughtful response, she lashed out and stormed off, stubborn and certain she was right.

With that attitude, this wouldn't be the last time she needed my help. I was sure of it. And for some reason, the thought of being there to protect her made me smile.

CHAPTER SIX

Kara

This party wasn't like the last one.

Music throbbed around me, but something about it didn't seem right. It was too loud. Or too fast. Or...

...something.

Whatever it was, it made the room spin. Somewhere close, or maybe far away, it was so hard to tell, someone laughed and the sound echoed weirdly. Todd Hudgins, captain of the football team, the star of every teenaged fantasy I'd ever had, and all-around master of the universe, leaned in close, nuzzling my ear. I flinched away from the contact, confused by my own slow thoughts.

"Come on, baby. Why so uptight?"

He thinks you're just like your mom, whispered an insidious voice in my head.

When Todd had invited me to this party, I was ecstatic. Three hours after arriving in a cloud of popularity and high-fives, the novelty was wearing off. Fast.

"Did you put something in my drink?" I pulled out of his grasp and stared into my red Solo cup, supposedly filled with plain old Coke. My words slurred and I wrinkled my brow, smelling something decidedly alcoholic.

"So what if I did? I thought you were cool with that kind of stuff."

"Damn it, Todd! What's in my drink?" The world set off spinning again as I lurched into a standing position. Despite the drug Kingpin reputation I had earned at Ryan's party last month, I had never so much as sipped a beer.

"What's it matter, baby?" Todd gripped my arms and pulled me back to the sofa. "Come back to papa and let me make you feel better."

Even through the haze of whatever I had ingested, his line was too cheesy to ignore. Todd Hudgins was supposed to be, like, a decent guy. A unicorn with good looks, good grades, and good manners.

I shrugged out of his grasp and stumbled for the door, sloshing the contents of my cup all over my shirt in the process. Whatever was in there, it definitely didn't smell like Coke. In fact, it smelled a lot like Burke when he came in for a hug. How did I not notice before?

"I should have known better than to think you were cool!" Todd called after me. "I'll teach you to waste my time, you stupid cunt!" And just like that, all my illusions about him crumbled, proving once again that the whole world was intent on letting me down.

I saw his brilliant smile for what it was: a way to lure girls like me into doing things they would regret. His sweet words were traps. The goal? One thing and one thing only, getting into my pants. Or anyone's pants. His blonde hair, his high school stardom, they were all wasted on him. Todd Hudgins, the golden boy, was nothing but a dickhead after all.

Drunk on shattered expectations and whatever it was he had slipped into my drink, I staggered through the clumps of inebriated teenagers, looking for a friendly face. Todd had driven me here and there was no chance I'd be getting back into a car with him. Brooke was on a weekend trip with her family, so calling in the cavalry was a no-go.

As much as I didn't want to reach out to Mom, she was looking more and more like my only chance of not having to walk home. The car ride would be nothing but thinly veiled barbs about how totally unfun I was for pulling her away from whatever she was doing on a Friday night, but it would be better than spending one more second here.

I locked myself in a bathroom, dug out my phone, and sent her a text. Ten minutes later, I sent another. Five minutes after that, I sent one more. Finally, I sent what I thought would be the holy grail of cries for help. It took me three tries to get it right. My fingers weren't listening to my brain.

MOM. I'm stuck at a party. This guy spiked my drink and tried to take advantage of me. I need help. Please.

As the minutes ticked by without a response and someone started banging on the bathroom door, the low hum of panic in my belly detonated into full-blown fear. I wanted to go home and I wanted to go home now. If my own mother wouldn't come save me, who else could I turn to?

The banging grew more insistent. "Come on!" someone called through the door. "You've been in there for like an hour or something."

I glanced at the time, adding up how long it had been since I locked myself in the overly bright room. Not quite an hour. But close. And not a peep from Mom. My thoughts were clearing up, but my stomach was not. Nausea grew with each passing minute, a coiled snake in my belly, slithering with the promise of vile things and ruined reputations. I did *not* want to be that girl who couldn't hold her liquor and threw up at a party.

I scrolled through my contacts, pausing to hurl an insult at the now constant doorbanger, and stopped when I came across the two entries for Burke Hutton. One was the phone he bought just to answer Mom's calls. The other, the one marked DO NOT USE UNDER ANY CIRCUMSTANCE, was his personal cell. It hadn't made sense when Mom gave me the number, though nothing about her ever did.

I sent a series of texts to his burner. Then tried calling. Then, in a moment of desperation as the guy on the other side of the door got downright mad, I called Burke's personal cell.

It rang once.

Then twice.

I sent out a silent prayer as it rang a third time. And as it finished the fourth ring, a rush of guilt washed over me, only to be chased by relief when someone picked up.

"What the hell are you doing calling this number?"

The disdain I heard could only mean I was talking to one person. "Wyatt! Wait! Please don't hang up." Even to my ears, I sounded like a desperate child and in that moment, I wasn't even ashamed. "I really need your help." Nausea churned in my stomach and I was afraid I might start crying.

I waited for the scathing response but when none came and the line stayed open, I launched into my story. "I really need a ride home," I finished. "I don't know what he put in my drink, I don't feel so good, and I'm really afraid."

After a long pause, Wyatt sighed. "Where are you?"

Relief surged through me because I could hear concern in his voice. Outside of Brooke, I couldn't remember the last time someone sounded concerned about me. "I locked myself in the bathroom."

"Good. Stay there. Text me the address." He hung up and I did as he said, then covered my face with my hands and waited, my head pounding in time with the asshole on the other side of the door.

Wyatt didn't make me wait long. Just a few minutes later, his deep voice boomed my name over the music and laughter of the party. I waited for the sound to get closer, then unlocked the bathroom door and pushed past the impatient kid standing on the other side with a murmured apology, staggering as I called Wyatt's name.

He took one look at me and wrapped an arm around my waist, pulling me close and guiding me toward the door. "You smell like a liquor cabinet." He sounded angry. Accusatory. I wanted to shoot back a caustic response, but I was too grateful. He rescued me when no one else would and that had little bombs of gratitude going off in my belly.

"I'm sorry," I mumbled as we stepped outside, taking a deep breath of fresh air, hoping my stomach would calm down now that I was safe.

He stayed silent as he guided me down the street to his car, helping me inside, then leaning through the passenger door to latch my seatbelt even though I could have done it myself. His scent permeated my space and I breathed him in.

"You smell good."

It took a second to realize I had spoken out loud, and by the time it registered, a throbbing headache devoured whatever embarrassment I might have felt. I leaned my head against the headrest, groaning. This might go down as the single worst night in my existence, even worse than the one that ended up with me in jail, and that was saying a lot.

Under the dome light, Wyatt's lips twitched with the ghost of a smile. "How much did you drink tonight?"

"I don't know." I swallowed hard. "I thought I was only drinking Coke, but obviously there was more in it. Don't know how I didn't notice the change in taste."

"He probably added a little more whisky every

time you turned your back. Specifically so you wouldn't taste it." Wyatt shook his head and shut my door before crossing in front of the car to climb into the driver's seat. He sat there, his hands gripping the steering wheel so hard his knuckles went white.

"Are you mad at me?" I asked.

An emotion I couldn't name flickered across his face. "I'm mad, but not at you. Not really." He ran a hand along the back of his neck. "I thought I told you to stop putting yourself in these situations."

"Putting myself in these situations?" The force of my indignation had my head lurching off the headrest, an action I immediately regretted, but I couldn't let Wyatt blame *me* for what happened tonight. "Because I *asked* Todd to spike my drink and take advantage of me?"

"Did he drag you to the party?"

"No. I came willingly."

"And did you keep an eye on your cup the whole night? Or might it, by chance, have gone unattended for some time?"

Suddenly hot, I leaned my head against the cool glass of the window. I had definitely left my cup unattended, but again, not my fault. I shouldn't have to pay that much attention when all I wanted was to have a little fun.

"And who knows where you are?" Wyatt continued. "Your Mom? Any friends?"

"Like telling my mom would have done any good." My breath fogged up the glass and I seriously regretted everything that led to this moment. The last thing I needed was a lecture from some guy who knew nothing about me. Wyatt was probably a Todd Hudgins when he was my age. Good looking. Charming. And toxic.

"I'm just saying..." Wyatt spoke with a strange mix of irritation and kindness. "You seem to think these things keep happening to you, but you're an active participant. You are making choices that allow you to be taken advantage of."

"Oh. So, because I came to a party with a boy, that makes it my fault when he turns out to be a shithead." I swallowed hard. My frustration with Wyatt churned in my stomach, adding to the already significant nausea. Go figure, I could add misogynistic asshole and victim-blamer to his long line of indiscretions.

"Nope." Wyatt glared out the windshield toward the house. "That one's on him. It's not your responsibility to make him honorable. But, you're the one who came to a party when you knew there wouldn't be any adults around. And after what happened last time, I would have hoped you learned your lesson. But you didn't. Instead, you made the same mistake, then added to it by not keeping an eye on your drink..."

I was so mad, I just wanted him to shut up and drive. Who did he think he was? Lecturing me when I hadn't done anything wrong. "Go ahead and blame the victim. Whatever makes you feel better, dude."

"Damn it, Kara! It's not your fault. But if you don't pay attention to the choices you made that led up to that guy taking advantage of you, then you'll just keep repeating this pattern. And one of these days I won't be here to rescue you."

"I don't need rescued."

Wyatt simply arched an eyebrow, then started the car.

After a few minutes of driving, I started to feel bad. Sometimes—okay, most times—I was too hotheaded for my own good. Wyatt deserved a little more gratitude and a lot less anger. "Look. What I meant to say was thank you for coming to get me."

He nodded, but wouldn't look at me.

Uncomfortable in the awkward silence, I continued, "What do you think he put in my drink?"

"From the smell of you, I'd say about half a bottle of Jim Beam."

He fell silent once again and I was too focused on trying not to vomit to keep restarting the conversation.

"You good?" Wyatt asked as he pulled up in front

of the condo. "Think you can make it inside or do you need help?"

I swallowed hard as nausea sent a rush of saliva into my mouth. I was definitely not good. Wyatt took one look at me and leapt into action, lurching out of the car, and yanking my door open. "Come on, Kara. I've got you." He helped me stand and the jostling and bouncing drew a long moan past my lips.

"I don't feel so great."

Wyatt murmured soothing words as he helped me to the front door of the condo. Panic rose into my throat, with whatever had happened to me at the party coming up right after it. The moment the door swung open, I ran in the direction of the bathroom, barely making it to the floor in front of the toilet before my stomach rid itself of an entire evening's worth of booze.

Wyatt held my hair and rubbed my back, then got me a drink of water. "You have any ibuprofen?" he asked as I clutched the wall.

I pointed a shaking finger at the medicine cabinet. He retrieved the bottle, then handed me two pills, made me sip some more water, then stuck around for another bout of vomiting before helping me into bed.

"Wyatt?" I asked as I pulled the covers up around me.

"Yeah?"

"You're the only one who came to help."

It was a thing of importance.

A thing I wouldn't forget.

When I needed him, he was there, even if he was an asshole about the whole thing and I was a bitch in return. The room spun and I closed my eyes, but I swore he stared at me for several long minutes before I passed out.

CHAPTER SEVEN

Wyatt

Madeline was nowhere to be found and for as uncomfortable as I was staying in Kara's room, I couldn't justify leaving. What if she started getting sick again and didn't wake up? Just because the girl infuriated me on a level I couldn't understand didn't mean I wanted her to choke to death on her own vomit.

I helped Kara out of her shoes and tucked her into bed fully clothed. Her gratitude was sweet and innocent and went a long way towards easing my frustration at how stubborn and bullheaded she was. Poor thing was just stumbling from mistake to mistake with no one to look out for her. Part of me was proud to be the one who did.

She fell asleep within seconds and I had no idea what to do with myself. Camp out in her room? Hunt down her mom? Make a bed on the couch? Or just call it a night and make my way home?

That last idea was out of the question. I couldn't leave. And if the main point of me staying here was to make sure she was safe, then I would need to stay close. I took a seat in a chair and prepared myself for a long, sleepless night, swearing that the moment I heard Madeline come home, I'd be out of there.

I was furious at that asshole who spiked her drink. It had taken every ounce of control not to storm back into that party and...what? Beat up a teenager? I wasn't the kind of guy who spoke with his fists in the first place, but hitting a kid in the face was out of the question. Even if he did deserve it.

The slow addition of alcohol to a girl's drink wasn't a tactic I had ever used, but I knew enough guys that had. She was lucky he hadn't tried something more narcotic. Something that would have left her with zero memory of the night and a reputation she couldn't shake.

A girl who looked like her, with those gray eyes and that olive skin. That dark hair cascading down her back to a beautifully curved set of hips...this wouldn't be the last time she attracted the wrong kind of attention. There had to be some way to protect her, to give her the tools she needed to protect herself.

And then I realized what an idiot I was being, wasting energy worrying about her when she seemed hellbent on getting herself into trouble. I had barely known her a few months and this was the second time she needed me to come to her rescue. How many times had she needed rescued before she knew me? Was she a perpetual damsel in distress? Playing the victim so hard she didn't even recognize she had some measure of responsibility in what happened to her?

Or, given what I knew of her mother, maybe Kara was an actual damsel in distress, bumbling through life with zero parental guidance. Or worse, the guidance of the kind of woman who latched onto men with wives and money.

For a split second, I felt genuine concern for the girl, but the moment was short-lived, and I chalked it up to stress and fatigue.

———

The sound of a door slamming jolted me from sleep. I lifted my head, confused, until I remembered where I was. Kara's room was still dark and the clock on her bedside table read four-thirty. If she was going to throw up, she probably would have done it already, so I figured it was safe for me to leave. Besides, her mom was obviously home and making a racket in the kitchen, singing to herself while she banged plates and silverware onto the counter.

A real class act, I thought to myself. *Showing up this early in the morning then making enough noise to wake the dead while her daughter slept.*

I hadn't even processed the fact that Kara told me she tried to reach out to the woman for help and received nothing but silence in return. I already hated Madeline. If I thought too hard on her lack of parenting skills, I couldn't be sure I would keep my mouth shut when I saw her.

Steeling myself for the inevitable confrontation at the sight of a grown man slipping out of her teenaged daughter's bedroom, I headed toward the sound, making enough noise to alert Madeline to my approach so I didn't scare the shit out her as I came around the corner.

"Kara? That you, baby?" Judging by the slurred words, mother and daughter had similar nights.

"Umm...no." I stepped into the kitchen, my explanation at the ready, and a wide smile broke across Madeline's face.

"Well if it isn't Wyatt Hutton." She slowly closed the refrigerator and flicked on the overhead light, her heels clicking against the tile floor as she gave me the once-over.

"I know how this looks…" I began, already on the defensive.

"You don't have to explain to me, sugar. I told Kara you were interested in her. I'm just glad she finally took that stick out of her ass and made her move."

My jaw dropped. "You have it so wrong, I don't even know what to say. I am not interested in your little girl." I explained the night and the events that lead to me choosing to stay. "I just wanted to make sure she was safe. And now that you're here, I can be on my way." Though something made me wonder if Kara was ever safe, given Madeline's last statement.

Smooth as silk, the woman changed tracks. "That was incredibly sweet of you to make sure she was okay," she said, suddenly playing the concerned mother. "I don't know why she didn't call me."

"According to Kara, she did. Several times." I backed out of the kitchen, feeling less and less okay about leaving, though I couldn't find a rational reason as to why I would feel that way other than the woman set off my internal alarms.

Madeline thanked me again and walked me to the door, waving as I lowered myself into my car. As much as I was ready to get home and climb into bed, I couldn't make myself leave. I stared at the woman waving from the doorway, anxiety churning in my stomach. All I needed to do was put the car in gear and get the hell out of Dodge. I just...couldn't.

"Come on, Wyatt," I said as I drummed my fingers against the steering wheel. "These are not your clowns, and this is not your circus."

I couldn't shake the feeling that Kara was in danger. Or she would be in danger again. And for as much as she wanted to be seen as having it all together, it was clear she didn't. Cursing under my breath, I turned off the engine and climbed out of the car.

"I forgot something," I murmured to Madeline. "Mind if I go up and grab it?"

"Oh sure, sugar," she said in a voice that disgusted me. "Take your time."

I crept back into Kara's room and fished her phone out of her purse. "Wyatt?" Her groggy voice caught my attention. "What the hell you doin' with my phone?"

"I'm adding myself to your contacts. Just in case."

Kara nodded, her eyes already closed again. "Thank you," she murmured and she sounded so genuinely grateful, something shifted in my heart, making room for this girl I wanted to hate.

CHAPTER EIGHT

Kara

My head pounded. My stomach boiled. Sandpaper lined my throat and my eyes refused to open. I groaned and rolled onto my back, then groaned again as the whole world continued to roll. What fresh hell was this?

I managed to open my eyes and immediately squeezed them shut as light bombarded my poor, aching head. Todd Hudgins would pay for what he did to me last night. I didn't know when. And I didn't know how. But he wouldn't get away with whatever he did to make me feel like I had been run over by a semi-truck several times throughout the night.

When I finally managed to open my eyes, I found a

glass of water and two ibuprofen tablets sitting on my bedside table next to my phone. I stared for a minute, my hungover brain trying to figure out where they might have come from. While I appreciated the gesture, it seemed a little too 'aware' for Mom. Though the little voice inside, the one that always hoped she would grow up and realize how many mistakes she made with me, started whispering.

Maybe she finally got to her phone, it said. *Maybe she saw all those missed messages and the guilt goosed the maternal side of her I knew had to be buried in there somewhere, lost under all her selfish BS.*

As I sat up, fumbling for the pills, a flash of memory from last night derailed that train of thought. Wyatt had been here. He had helped me while I threw up—not once, but twice. And when I was done, he had helped me into bed. And, for some reason, I thought I remembered him standing over me in the middle of the night, messing with my phone.

The memory came fully into focus and I knew without a doubt that Mom hadn't been the one to leave the water and pills on my table. It had been Wyatt Hutton. After coming to rescue me at the party, after helping my drunk self out of his car, after having the balls to lecture me about *my* mistakes last night, after holding my hair and helping me upstairs, he had come back to put his number into my phone.

Just in case, he had said.

And at some point after I succumbed to sleep yet again, he left these things here so they would be waiting when I woke up. Because he knew I would need them. I flopped back onto my pillow, smiling like a crazy person at the thought of him taking care of me, though the smile faded as my mind churned.

I had no idea what to do with that bit of kindness and I certainly couldn't begin to unravel what it possibly meant, or what he thought he could get from me. Because let's be honest. He was the son of a lying, cheating drunk. Even though Burke was good to me, not many people could say the same and I was sure the apple didn't fall too far from the tree. With those thoughts swirling through my aching head, I took the pills and a long swig of water, then fell back to sleep.

Saturday was hard, compliments of my first ever hangover and a mom who was sure I had slept with Wyatt. I swore to her I hadn't, then let her know how much I needed her help the night before. "So, you know, thanks for being there," I finished, glaring at her as she nursed a hangover of her own.

"Oh, Poopsie. Don't you think you're a little too old to need your mommy to come rescue you?"

I poured myself a cup of coffee and leveled her with a cold stare. "That excuse might be valid if you hadn't used it on me since I was three years old."

Mom stormed off, locked herself in her bedroom, and didn't emerge again. I stared at my phone for a good hour before sending Wyatt a thank you text and almost jumped out of my skin when it buzzed with a reply immediately.

How are you feeling? Hanging in there?

I smiled as I tapped out a response. **I've seen better days.**

Did you find the water and the pills? The trick is to stay hydrated.

My smile brightened. **I did. I really appreciate you taking care of me last night. I know I was difficult, and I'm sorry for that. My friend says I have a warrior's spirit and sometimes it gets the better of me.**

My phone went silent for a few minutes, then buzzed again. **I'm glad I could help. You know where to find me if you need rescued again.**

I grinned wildly as I stared at the screen, then put down my phone and refilled my coffee.

I spent Sunday at the beach, so that kind of made up for Saturday, but Monday sucked hard. The rumor mill had been grinding away since I left Todd's side

Friday night and I spent the morning ignoring side-eyed whispers from half the school. For all my self-righteous fury the morning after the party, I had yet to figure out how to make the asshole pay. I didn't have the social clout he did. Which was fine. I had self-respect instead. What I didn't have was the respect of my classmates. Not anymore.

"So, what the hell happened this weekend?" Brooke plopped down beside me at the lunch table, her tray of French fries clattering against mine. "You slept with Todd Hudgins and didn't tell me?"

If the story was true, I would deserve the outraged tone, but it wasn't true, and Brooke should have known better. "*Et tu, Brute?*"

"Oh, lord help me," she said on a heavy sigh. "You know it's bad when you start quoting Shakespeare."

I rolled my eyes. "Come on now. Of all the people at this school, I thought I could trust you not to judge me before you heard the whole story. Do you really think I would do something so stupid, and then not bother to tell you?"

"Yeah. Actually, I do." Brooke twisted the cap off a water bottle and eyed me while taking a swig.

"Gee, thanks." I puffed out my cheeks, pretending to be blasé about her statement while a tiny voice chattered away in the back of my head.

She thinks you're just like your mom. You said it

yourself, after all. The apple doesn't fall far from the tree. If it's true about Wyatt, it could be true about you.

Brooke put her water bottle down and kicked my shin under the table. "You know I love you. *And* you know I don't really believe the story. And *you* know, that *I* know, if you slept with Todd Hudgins, I'd be the first to hear about it."

"Is that what they're saying?" I asked. "They all think I slept with him?" I had done my best to avoid the rumors, keeping my head down and my focus on my schoolwork.

Brooke scoffed. "I wish that was all they're saying."

The look on her face said it would be better for me if I stuck with my original policy of paying the rumors zero attention and getting on with my life. Which only made my curiosity burn brighter. I pressed and she finally relented.

"They're saying you sucked his dick in the living room, let him finger you in the kitchen, then fucked him on the stairs. And, they're saying you were a shitty lay."

I dropped my chin into my hands. "This one will be fun to live down."

"I don't think there's any living this one down." Brooke popped a fry into her mouth. "So, what really happened?"

I explained the events that led up to me locking

myself in the bathroom and Brooke shook her head. "I am so sorry I wasn't there for you."

"It's not your fault you were in Colorado with your family."

"No. But still. The first time you really needed my help and I was halfway across the country. After all the times you've helped me, it would have felt good to return the favor."

I wanted to point out that if she had been there, she would have been too wasted to be of any use, hence, all the times I had to be the one helping her. I let that point slide, though. Brooke meant well, even if she didn't see herself honestly.

"How did you get home?" she asked, pausing to wave at someone over my shoulder. "Did your mom actually prove herself useful and come get you?"

I laughed. "Uh. No. I had to call one of her boyfriends."

Brooke's eyes widened. "And *he* came to get you?"

"Wrong again. The boyfriend's son came to my rescue."

Again, I finished in my head.

I found myself explaining everything that led up to me discovering the water and pills on my table Saturday morning, followed by the addition of his contact info in my phone. "I can't figure it out," I finished, as I tried for the hundredth time to see Wyatt's angle.

Brooke scrunched up her nose. "Figure what out?"

"What he wants." I stabbed at my food. "We had this perfectly fine thing going where we hated each other. So, what's with the nice stuff all the sudden?"

"Maybe...I don't know...he's a decent guy? And maybe he sees your mom for what she is and since he's had to rescue you twice now, he decided to skip the middle man and just give you his phone number so you could call him directly the next time?"

"First of all, thanks for assuming there's gonna be a next time. And second of all, I'm not buying it. No one is nice unless they want something."

Not my mom.

Not Todd Hudgins.

And not Wyatt Hutton.

Brooke punched me in the shoulder. "I'm someone."

"Huh?"

"I'm someone. And I'm nice to you. And all I want is your scintillating company."

"See?" I said, holding up a finger. "Point proven. You're nice because you want something, just like everyone else in the world." I grinned and she rolled her eyes.

Brooke returned her focus to her food while I

worried about the utter destruction of what little reputation I had. Not that it mattered all that much. I really
didn't care what anyone at that school thought about
me. I'd be out of here the second I turned eighteen and
Todd Hudgins and all his stupid friends could rot.

"What's he look like?" Brooke asked, interrupting
my thoughts. "Your mother's boyfriend's son? Is he
hot?"

That word didn't do him justice. It was too
simple. Too juvenile. Too pop culture. Wyatt Hutton
had a strength and grace that transcended those
things. His sex appeal was timeless and didn't fit into
a single label. Even his overprotective nature was
starting to do it for me...when it wasn't pissing me off
instead.

"Does it matter?" I asked.

"It always matters."

Wyatt's sea glass eyes came into my mind. His
broad shoulders. His warm smile and the furrowed
brow that ate away at it whenever we were together.
"It's not what's on the outside that counts."

Brooke threw her head back, hooting in laughter
and drawing the curious glances of a gaggle of girls a
table over. "That means he's gorgeous, but you don't
like him and won't admit it."

I set out with the intention of hating Wyatt, but
now, I couldn't exactly explain how I felt about him.

Hate was certainly the wrong word, but had things changed so much that I could say I liked him?

"It doesn't matter how good looking he is," I replied. "He's older than me."

"How much older?"

I told Brooke his age and her eyebrows hit her hairline. "Yeah, just a little too old for us, huh?"

In that moment, I wanted to hug her. My mom's reaction to the difference in our ages had me questioning my sanity. The fact that Brooke also felt uncomfortable with Wyatt being twenty-one made me feel a little saner. A little more like I wasn't an eighty-five-year-old woman trapped in a teenager's body. Mom had me wondering if I was being a prude. Was a five-year age gap not really that big of a deal?

It felt huge to me. All the things I had yet to experience, big things, life-altering things, they were old hat to Wyatt. Though, after last weekend, I could officially say I had been wasted. And that I had survived a massive hangover. My list of big, life-altering things I had yet to live through was shrinking down to only include experiences with boys.

First kisses...

First loves...

Wyatt's face came to mind and I wasn't sure how I felt, having him connected to ideas like kissing and love.

CHAPTER NINE

Wyatt

A month passed, and Harlow's sixteenth birthday right along with it. The family celebrated the occasion with a huge cake in the shape of a car, lots of stories about life with her, and gifts galore. Lucas joined in via Skype, and Dad took the time to make sure she was aware how often she let him down.

Every time someone had something good to say, every time she so much as smiled, he pointed out some failing of hers. Real or imagined, it didn't matter. He railed at her for her art work. Her sensitivity. Her lack of interest in anything he thought would lead to a 'proper job.'

I had been afraid we would lose her for days after

that, but for some reason, Dad's comments didn't seem to affect her. She had been lighthearted and happy and *present* in the several weeks since her birthday and it made my heart glad.

Today, I watched her through the dining room window as she sat at the edge of the dock, her feet swinging in the water and her eyes on the setting sun. Her white-blonde hair shone with a light of its own and before I had too much time to think about it, I let myself outside and made my way to the dock.

"Hey there," she said, glancing up as I sat beside her. "To what do I owe this pleasure?"

"I saw you out here and thought it looked like a nice place to spend an evening."

Harlow beamed. "It really is. If you sit still enough, you can hear so much in the silence between the waves." She glanced at me, checking to see if I was going to verbally smack her down for saying something dumb.

Instead, I smiled. "Sometimes I wish I could see the world the way you do."

"What's that mean?" She wrinkled her brow and returned her focus to the water.

"It means that I think you see more than the average person." I shrugged. "I don't know. Sounds a little dumb when I say it out loud."

"It doesn't." Harlow bumped a shoulder against

mine. "It's actually a relief to hear you say that because that's exactly how I feel sometimes. Like I see how things are connected and I understand how people are feeling before they even figure it out for themselves."

"Yeah? Then how am I feeling right now?"

Harlow took one look at me and spoke a truth I wasn't prepared for. "Worried."

That one word hit me hard. I expected her to say I was happy, because that was how I felt. Or that she would choose to go with a joke, because that was how we liked to relate to each other. But worried? That one caught me off guard.

"Worried about what?" I asked.

"Well, maybe a little about me, since you came out here to sit next to me like a creeper." She grinned as she gave me the joke I was expecting. "But, I don't know, it seems like you've been off lately. Your smile doesn't reach your eyes anymore, Wy-guy."

"I don't know about all that," I said, brushing off the statement before turning the focus back to her. "Anyway, I just wanted you to know I've been impressed with you."

"Right. Because I'm such an impressive specimen."

Self-degradation was a defense mechanism, one we'd all adopted, but Harlow had it down to a science.

"That's not true and you know it," I said. She was good at everything she did. "I'm impressed because

Dad was such a jerk to you on your birthday. And in the past, that would have hit you hard and the last place I would have found you was here, in your happy place."

"This is true." Harlow bobbed her head in agreement.

"So, what changed?"

She gave me a quiet smile. "I realized I can't please him. Never have. Never will. And somehow, that realization was freeing. I've spent so much of my life trying to trim off the parts of myself that he hates, and like, I basically would have to keep trimming until there was nothing left. If I stop trying to please him, I can just be myself. And it feels really good."

I stared at my sister, looking for something uplifting to say while anger crept through my veins. Harlow was a good person, sensitive and loyal, the kind of girl who would give up something she loved just to make someone else happy. The fact that Dad refused to see her for what she was infuriated me. "He's really not worth your time," I said.

"I'm starting to realize that. It's just...you and he are so close. And Lucas always tells stories about how he used to be...you know, before he started drinking. Part of me wishes I could know him like you guys do. The other part is glad you don't know him the way I do."

Harlow thought I was close to Dad? How could she think that? The answer slapped me in the face before I was done asking myself the question. Thanks to our little secret, I was probably the closest one to him, the one who knew him better than anyone else in our family. The realization brought a surge of anger—at him, at myself, at Madeline and Kara—and I did my best to hide it from Harlow.

"Sometimes," I murmured, "it feels like the man he is murdered the man he used to be. I don't want him to turn his focus on anyone else." Because I couldn't stand to lose another family member the way I lost my dad.

"And you take the brunt of it so we don't have to."

I shrugged and Harlow continued.

"Maybe that's why your smile doesn't reach your eyes anymore. Maybe he's killing you, the same way he killed himself."

I broke eye contact and cleared my throat, before wrapping an arm around my sister's shoulder. "I'm just glad to see you feeling confident," I said before making up some excuse about needing to run an errand and wandering back to the house.

Dad wasn't home.

And I knew where he was.

Today was Kara's seventeenth birthday, and while he brought nothing but condescension to Harlow's party, he had a slew of gifts for another man's daughter.

With Harlow's words swimming through my mind—
maybe he's killing you, the same way he killed himself—
I swiped my keys off the counter and drove to Madeline's condo.

I couldn't keep doing this. I couldn't keep his
secrets from our family. I couldn't fund his affair,
finding more and more creative ways to hide the
missing money. If I was going to stay true to myself, if I
was going to survive, I needed to end our little
arrangement.

As I drove, a battle waged inside me. My conscious
versus his sneaky words.

*If this secret ever comes out, it will ruin this
family.*

*Your mother needs The Hut, and without the
family, The Hut will die.*

The family is more important than your morals.

*If you tell them what we've been doing, you'll lose
them all.*

By the time I pulled to a stop in front of the condo,
I was so twisted up, I didn't know what to do. The urge
to push through the front door and tell him I was done
was so strong, I couldn't catch my breath. My hands
were fists. My jaw was tight. None of this anger felt
natural to me. I had no experience with it, and therefore, had no idea what to actually do with it. My
thoughts were tangled and filled with thorns, preparing

to tell Dad he could stuff his lies into his whisky and drown in it.

It was at that exact moment that the front door swung open and Kara stepped out. She stopped in her tracks when her eyes fell on mine, then laughed as she lowered herself to sit on the front step. "Ahhh. If it isn't my favorite stalker," she said as I got out of the car. "Come here to wish me a happy birthday?"

"Not exactly." I shrugged and shoved my hands into my back pockets.

She bobbed her head then patted the spot beside her. "Keep me company? Our parents are...uh...celebrating."

Of course they were. Because what else could you do on a child's birthday but kick her out of the house. Though, one look at Kara confirmed she was no child...

I refused to finish that thought. It was dangerous to think that way, especially given how beautiful she looked that night.

"I'm sorry about them," I said as I closed the distance between us, each step making me more and more aware of how much I wanted to talk to her. She'd had my number for a month now and sent the odd text here or there, random things about school or memes she found funny. Those conversations would be followed by long stretches of silence and, strangely enough, I wished she would text more. Initiating the contact myself was out of the question. The girl was too young.

"Don't apologize for them." Kara waved toward the door. "I'm used to that kind of BS. Even the things that are about me, aren't actually about me." She smirked and I sat, keeping a fair amount of space between us. "Why are you here, big guy?"

I let out a long breath, and before I knew what was happening, I told her everything. I explained my sister and her tumultuous relationship with our dad. I explained how angry I was on behalf of my mom and siblings, how I wasn't built for that kind of constant lying and manipulation. The only thing I didn't explain was how good it felt to sit next to her.

"I came here tonight to tell him to go fuck himself. That I was done keeping his secret."

Kara wrapped her arms around her torso, her hands gripping her biceps while her elbows rested on her knees. "And yet, he's in there and you're out here." She pursed her lips. "Funny."

I prickled at the challenge in her statement and sighed. She was right. My grand plan to confront my father had stalled out right here on her front steps.

"See," she said. "That's why I'm leaving as soon as I hit eighteen."

Her words reminded me of Caleb, and then Eli who promised the same thing. "Why's that?" I asked, while I wondered if she and I had more in common than I cared to admit.

"I've got money and big dreams. I'm not sticking around to let my mom and her craziness keep on ruining my life."

"What kind of big dreams?"

Kara ran a hand through her hair and gathered it over her shoulder. "Don't laugh at me?"

"I would never laugh at a person for trying to make a better life for themselves." *Especially when that someone is you*, I thought but didn't say.

"I make jewelry," Kara began, then explained her obsession with taking stones and metal and turning them into something beautiful. "I want to get out of the Keys and open a business, selling the things I make..." She trailed off, fear of judgement dancing in her eyes.

She sounded so naïve. So unaware of herself and the world. I resisted the urge to say that to her, though. It was her birthday. For as much as I resented her for getting all the attention Harlow deserved, it wasn't lost on me that Kara was sitting outside on the front stoop, alone as far as the people inside knew. Maybe she didn't get any more from Burke Hutton than the rest of us, but compared to what she got from her mom, it was enough.

I found myself feeling grateful for my mom and my siblings, for the support they offered me. I also found myself wanting to be that for Kara, though she felt less and less like a little sister and more and more like...

Stop it. Stop it right now. You can't finish that thought with your integrity intact.

She was a child and I was a man and if I did what I came here to do, I wouldn't be seeing her anymore. And so, we sat in silence as the sun began its slow-motion trek toward the horizon. The sky caught fire. It reflected in Kara's eyes and she looked up and caught me staring.

"You don't have to stick around, you know." She fiddled with the hem of her shorts. "I'm a big girl. I can take care of myself."

She stared at me, her eyes wide and innocent. She looked young. And alone. And so beautiful I couldn't think straight. "I'm sure you can," I replied, glancing away. "But no one should have to spend their birthday by themselves." An idea struck me and I spoke before I had time to think better of it. "We don't have to sit out here on the step, you know. You feel like going some-where? We can celebrate in style..." I felt foolish as I offered the suggestion, but that faded as gratitude warmed Kara's eyes.

"That's very sweet of you," she said, waving as a pair of headlights swung around the corner. "But I already have plans."

I had a dark thought. One about that boy at the

party. The one who spiked her drink. If that car pulled up with a guy behind the wheel, I didn't think I could let her go with him. Which was ridiculous. Who was I to decide what she could and couldn't do?

A Volkswagen Beetle pulled up and a blonde poked her head out the open window. "Hey sweet birthday girl! You ready for a torrid night of debauchery and bad decisions?"

Kara lifted a hand in greeting. "Always!" she called to her friend as she stood, then paused to bend down and kiss me on the cheek. "Thanks for keeping me company, big guy" she said with a smile that lit up her whole face. "Truly."

"Any time," I replied then watched as she bounded down the steps and got in the car.

CHAPTER TEN

Kara

Brooke gave me a wild look as I lowered myself into the passenger seat. Her gaze darted over my shoulder to land on Wyatt who still stood on the front steps, then came right back to me. I braced myself for the incoming barrage of questions and my best friend did not disappoint.

She flicked on her indicator and then just sat there, staring at me expectantly. "That's him, isn't it? Your mother's boyfriend's son? And for fucks sake, what's his name because that's a mouthful and we're going to be talking about him a lot."

"Wyatt," I murmured. "His name is Wyatt and yeah, that's him." And if I had anything to say about it, we wouldn't be talking about him at all. After surviving that charged atmosphere and my constant desire to touch him, I needed time to get my thoughts in order before handing them to Brooke.

She turned to me with wide eyes. "What's he doing at your house?"

I shrugged off the question. "Since it's my birthday, I humbly request that we please talk about something else. Any other topic would be perfectly acceptable."

"Nope." Brooke shook her head again as she finally navigated onto the street. "I'm sorry. We absolutely cannot talk about anything other than that man. He is officially the only thing I want to discuss with you for the rest of the night."

"It's going to be a quiet night then." The evening with Wyatt had unnerved me. He seemed so genuine. So confused as to how to deal with Burke.

He also smelled very good and every time I looked into his eyes, it was more and more difficult to look away. I fell into their depths, drowning in feelings and sensations I didn't understand. I spent the whole time fighting the urge to close the distance between us. To take his hand and rub my fingers along the rough edges of his knuckles. My gaze kept falling to his lips and I'd find myself wondering how they would taste. Of all the possible first kisses, having mine come from Wyatt Hutton suddenly seemed like a fantastic turn of events.

"Why was he there?" Brooke glanced my way before giving her attention back to her driving. "Does he have a crush on you? Oh my God, he does. And I know I said he was too old, and really, he is, but look at him! There has to be some kind of clause in the rules for exceptional hotness, right?"

For a split second, I allowed myself to entertain the thought of a clause that made the difference in our ages less of a problem. A smile tugged at my lips, but I swallowed it away, reminding myself that Wyatt and I really didn't get along. Not at all. Whatever that was tonight was an anomaly.

"He showed up to tell off his dad, who was inside celebrating my birthday with my mom in their own special way."

"Eww..." Brooke scrunched up her nose and looked as appalled as I felt.

"That pretty much sums up my feelings on the subject."

"But he didn't go inside, did he? He stopped on the step, captivated by your beauty..." She put a hand to her heart. "The ravaged hero, rescuing his damsel in distress from her mother's exploits with nothing more than his company."

I was not a damsel in distress and nothing resembling a rescue happened on those steps. I needed space.

I provided myself said space. Wyatt just happened to be there.

"Brooke. Please. You have to stop. Wyatt might be gorgeous, but he and I are like oil and water."

"I'd say more like gasoline and a match." Brooke grinned. "I saw the way he was looking at you." She waved her hand like she burned it.

I sighed, chasing away laughter. "Can we please just get on with the torrid debauchery already?"

She glanced my way, then rolled her eyes. "Fine. Whatever the birthday girl wants, the birthday girl gets."

We drove through the streets, music blaring, hair streaming, and all the anxiety of the evening with Wyatt blowing away. We arrived at the beach in a cluster of other cars, people from school streaming out of them.

"Where are we?" I asked.

Brooke gave me a wide smile. "Ummm...our people call this the beach." She made a broad gesture toward the ocean.

"You think you're so funny," I said, laughing. "You know what I mean. I thought we were going to dinner."

"Going to Bricks & Mortar just sounded so...every day," she said as she killed the engine and turned to me. "You only turn seventeen once. I mean, it's the last birthday of your childhood. I figured a much larger celebration than pretentious pizza for two was in order."

"What did you do?" It touched me that of all the people in my life, Brooke was the one to make my birthday special.

Though, I thought, *sitting on the front porch with Wyatt was pretty special, too...*

That was enough of that. I made a promise to myself to banish that man from my head for the rest of the evening.

Brooke threw up her hands. "Surprise?" A question gleamed in her eyes as a crowd of kids yanked open the door and pulled me out, then dragged me onto the beach, chanting and screaming. Even the recent hit to my popularity thanks to Todd and his rumors couldn't outweigh the lure of a beach party.

These kids were here to have fun.

And so was I.

Brooke was right. This was the last birthday of my childhood and I decided to usher in my seventeenth year in a cloud of fun. When someone offered me a beer, I said yes. When someone else offered me another, I said yes again. And when I saw Todd Hudgins' Solo cup sitting at his side—unattended—I poured a little vodka in there, bit by bit, just like he had done to me.

When he lurched to his feet an hour later, drunk

and confused and whiny as hell, I laughed right along with the rest of crowd, catching Brooke's eyes and giving her a silent high-five.

———

Wyatt

I stood on Kara's front porch, staring at the road long after the car disappeared. The girl was going to get herself in trouble again. I knew it. I would go home and get into bed, only to receive a series of frantic text messages in the middle of the night because she was in some kind of situation she didn't know how to get herself out of. Again.

I considered hopping into my car and following her, rationalizing the urge by suggesting I could save myself a lot of trouble if I was there to catch whatever she was getting into while it was happening. But deep down, I knew I wanted to follow Kara because I couldn't stop worrying about her. The moment she got into that car, a million different scenarios started drifting through my head and all I knew was that I didn't want any of them to happen. Not because I didn't want to have to come to her rescue. But because

I didn't want her to have to suffer through any more hardships.

The more I got to know Kara, the more I wanted to know her. There was something about her I couldn't deny. She had gotten under my skin with her spunky bravado. The innocence she tried so desperately to hide. The quick intelligence gleaming through those gray eyes.

I ran a hand along the back of my neck, feeling miserable. Special or not, Kara was only seventeen. She was a child, and I was a man, and that meant she was off limits.

I cringed when a voice in my head whispered, *but only for another year.*

With thoughts like that filling my mind, I needed a distraction. Imagine my surprise when it came in the shape of my father.

"Wyatt?"

I turned at his voice, just as surprised to see him as he was to see me.

"What are you doing here?" he asked. "Where's Kara?"

"She left with her friend while you were...*busy.*"

Dad ran his hands through his hair and down the back of his neck. "Damn it. I hate the thought of her spending her birthday stuck out on the porch."

If I didn't know any better, I would have thought

Dad was feeling regret, or shame, or maybe some combination of the two and I didn't know what to do with that fact. I only knew how to deal with the hateful side of him.

"But you were here for her? Right?" Dad looked up, hopeful and obviously hating himself for it.

"I guess you could say that. I didn't exactly come to tell her happy birthday." I came to tell you off for celebrating her birthday. I came to tell you to take your secret and stuff it up your ass.

The family will crumble if you do.

Everyone will hate you.

And you'll be ruining Kara's life, too. No fancy home. No private school. Not if Dad stops paying for them.

The last thought was a kick to the gut and I tried to untangle it. Dad wouldn't stop being Dad just because I stopped doing what he told me to do. If he wanted to be with Madeline, he would. If he wanted to send Kara to school, he would. Standing up to him wouldn't hurt my family. It wouldn't hurt Kara. It would only hurt him....

"You'd be good for her," Dad said, taking me off guard.

"What?"

"Kara's a good kid. A little naïve. A little impulsive." He laughed to himself. "Okay, a lot impulsive..."

I crossed my arms over my chest. "Just what are you saying, here?"

"I'm saying you could look after her. That if you two got to know each other a little better..."

Part of me was immediately a fan of getting to know Kara a little better. The rest was concerned that Dad might be trying to hook me up with his mistress' daughter. Leave it to him not to see all the different levels of fucked up in that situation. "Seems like I've already been doing a lot of taking care of Kara. Rescuing her from jail. Picking her up from parties with douchebags..."

Dad frowned. "You picked her up from a party? Is that what that call was to my phone...?"

I waved off his concern. "I have to hand it to you. I didn't think you could get more fucked up than you already are. I didn't think you could pull me any further into your stupid web of crazy than you already had. But this? Trying to get me involved with a kid...?"

"She's not going to be a kid much longer, Wyatt."

"It doesn't matter! She's a kid now. And you're, what? Doing some weird paternal protection thing by trying to connect me to her?"

"I think you could be good for her."

I turned away from my dad. The whole point of coming here tonight was for me to tell him I was done.

To put distance between me and him, and therefore also to put distance between myself and Kara.

He cleared his throat. "Seems like she could teach you a thing or two, as well. About standing up for yourself. About seeing the world for what it is and not what you want it to be. Kara's tough."

"And I'm not?"

Dad blew a puff of air through his nose and I had to take a long, uncomfortable look at myself. I didn't like what I saw. Not one bit. And it was time to start acting like the kind of man I wanted to be.

"I'm moving out," I said, barely aware I had made the decision before I spoke the words.

"Wyatt..."

"No. I mean it. I just...need some space to breathe. I'll still be at The Hut every day for work." And to protect mom and the two siblings left at home from Dad. "And I'll still keep your secret. But the more we're together, the more I feel like I'm turning into you."

"Would that be such a bad thing?"

"Have you seen yourself?" I saw him more and more clearly with each passing minute. The man I once admired was truly gone.

Dad huffed and set his jaw. "I'm a successful businessman. I raised a family while carving out our name

and building our wealth. I'm in the prime of my life. I'm smart. Driven."

"You're deceitful and cruel."

He shook his head. "You don't understand."

"I do. I understand more than you give me credit for. You had everything and you've just been pissing it away. Day by day. Drink by drink."

"That's enough," Dad barked.

"You're right. It is." Without another word, I stalked off the front porch and into my car.

The next day, I started looking for houses.

The next week, I moved into one.

CHAPTER ELEVEN

KARA

Mom's backup guy sat too close to me on our plush leather couch. I shifted, trying to create more space between us, but every time I moved, he somehow managed to get closer. "Mom should be back soon," I said, shifting yet again. "I'm just gonna head to my room and get some studying done."

I stood and the creep grabbed my wrist, tugging me back down beside him. "She won't be back all that soon. You know how your mom is. Come on, baby. Relax."

His words echoed in my head, reminding me of Todd Hudgins when he spiked my drink, and awakening that awful voice that hid in the back of my head.

He thinks you're just like your mom.

"Don't call me that." I yanked on my wrist, but he tightened his grip. "Let go of me!" I cried as his fingers bruised my flesh.

He leaned in, his breath hot on my lips. "I like a girl with fight."

This was it.

My first kiss was going to be stolen from me by a man more than twice my age.

I turned my head and his lips grazed my cheek, then caught in my hair. His free hand fondled a breast, squeezing cruelly before he gripped my jaw, forcing my face back to his.

"Stop it," I managed through clenched teeth.

The harder I struggled, the bigger he seemed, his body covering mine, making it impossible to move. Rage chased tears out of my eyes, which only seemed to fuel his desire.

"That's right. Cry for me, baby." His erection pressed into my hip.

Instead of crying, I screamed as loud as I could, struggling harder and harder against him, because it didn't matter what he thought, I was nothing like my mom. Just before I managed to break free, the asshole slapped me. Pain seared across my cheek and my head spun.

"Shut! Up!" he screamed.

A knock sounded at the door and hope bloomed in my chest.

I shrieked for help, but the guy covered my mouth with his hand. I struggled to yell again, desperate to make whoever was out there hear me.

"Kara?" Wyatt's voice, muffled through the door. I sagged in relief.

Sinking my teeth into the asshole's hand, I pulled away and yelled Wyatt's name. In a flash, he was through the front door, dragging Backup Guy off me.

"What the fuck do you think you're doing?" Wyatt asked, his words a razor.

"We're just having a little fun." Backup Guy drew his hand across his lips and I saw blood dripping from the bitemark I left on his palm.

"Where you having fun?" Wyatt asked me.

I shook my head, unable to find my voice.

"She says she wasn't having any fun," Wyatt said, and the look on his face was a gun, cocked, loaded, and pointed at the asshole's temple.

Backup Guy stammered a series of excuses and a cloud of rage distorted Wyatt's features. He grabbed the guy by his shirt, dragged him through the living room, and threw him outside. The man landed in a lump, grunting as he tumbled down the concrete stairs.

Wyatt closed the door and turned to me. "Are you okay?" He stayed where he was, an entire room separating us, as if I was a wild animal he didn't want to frighten away.

I started to nod. Of course I was okay. I was Kara Lockhart and I could handle myself. At least that's what I wanted the world to think. The truth was a little less grandiose. Instead of answering, my face crumbled and I ran into his embrace, pressing my head into his chest. He wrapped his arms around me and I sobbed, the terror of the incident finally catching up. He held me as if he could shield me from the world. When I got a hold of myself, I pulled away, wiping my face and apologizing.

Wyatt leaned down, searching out eye contact. "Hey. Look at me. Are you okay? Did he hurt you?" He placed a finger under my chin and turned my face, inspecting me for signs of damage.

I could feel the angry red print of Backup Guy's palm burning on my cheek. I knew his blood still coated my chin from where I bit him. But that wasn't the kind of hurt Wyatt was asking about.

I shook my head. "He didn't..." I choked on the words, then tried again. "There wasn't any..." Images of what the guy might have done to me had adrenaline rocketing through my veins and I stopped trying to finish the sentence. So much more than my first kiss had been at stake.

Wyatt nodded and didn't press any harder. "Come

on, sweet girl. Let's get you cleaned up." The nickname touched me and I had to fight another rush of tears. Damn Backup Guy for making me so emotional. Or maybe it was Wyatt with his solid strength and resolve. I felt safe enough to let down my guard with him. I wasn't sure that was a good thing.

"That was another one of Mom's boyfriends," I said, offering him an apologetic glance as he dabbed at my face with a damp cloth in the kitchen. I wondered if he knew my mom wasn't exclusive to his dad, then realized it didn't matter. I was tired of her messed up decisions having anything to do with my life.

Wyatt nodded, his face severe and unreadable. "Where is your mom?"

"She left just before he got here. Said she had some errands to run and that she would be right back."

Wyatt nodded, then sighed. "I'm just glad I got here when I did."

So was I, but I couldn't bring myself to say it out loud because I wasn't just glad he arrived to save me from Backup Guy. Simply being near him had my heart feeling lighter. His protective nature, usually so overbearing and frustrating, made me feel safe. Cared for. I had the sense that everything was going to be okay and I never felt that way. Every choice I made had an undercurrent of panic running through it.

I had no idea what I was doing in life and was

making a giant mess of it all. Time and again, Wyatt was there when I needed him, helping me put things back together. He resented me for it. And I resented him a little, too. I didn't like having my flaws on display and he seemed to see them all.

He met my eyes and I almost drowned in what I saw there. "Are you sure you're okay?" he asked again.

"I'm fine. Nothing hurts but my dignity." And my faith in humanity. Seemed like everywhere I looked, someone was busy ruining any hope I had for the state of society.

Men wanted women for one thing: sex.

And women wanted men for one thing: money.

In that moment, I swore to myself that I would be different. I would rather be alone than live a life that resembled my mother's in any way. I would stand on my own two feet and no man would ever use me for anything. Not for sex. Not for power. I would earn everything I had, even if that meant I had very little.

As those thoughts streamed through my head, tears reformed in my eyes. Before I knew what was happening, they started slipping down my cheeks. Wyatt wiped one away, nothing but sympathy in his gaze.

"It just feels like there's no hope, you know?" I wiped away the tears, angry at myself for letting them fall. "Like everywhere I turn, I find people who want to take something from me. The world is a cruel place." I shrugged. "Why let anyone in? They're only going to hurt me."

Wyatt nodded, studying me thoughtfully, then let out a long breath through his nose. I could see he was about to say something and I suddenly felt stupid for opening myself up to him.

"Never mind," I said as I hopped onto the counter. "I'm sure you're only going to blame me for what just happened. You know, since that's what you like to do. Blame the victim."

"I'm not blaming you." Wyatt leaned against the fridge, folding his arms across his chest.

"Excuse me?" I blinked in mock confusion, donning sarcasm like a suit of armor. "Come again?"

"No blame. None. This one wasn't on you. You shouldn't have been left alone with that guy. And he... well. He is a waste of space and the air he breathes."

Wyatt's face twisted with anger and for the first time all of his judgmental speeches made sense. He hadn't been condemning me, he had been worried about me. That realization awakened a feeling of such vulnerability, I yearned to have my defensive walls falling back into place around my heart. I didn't like being this open. If felt raw and dangerous and I was sure to end up hurt.

And yet...

...and yet...

There was something beautiful about being unguarded with him. About trusting him with my poor trembling heart and knowing he wouldn't leave it smashed to bits.

"You can say that again." I tried to sound cool. Calm. Collected. Like a strong, independent woman who could handle such injustices with little more than a laugh and a promise to take the man's balls the next time she saw him. Instead, my voice wobbled and cracked, betraying my anxiety. I dropped off the counter, hoping he hadn't heard my emotions on display. "Hey," I said. "I have something for you."

Before he could say a word, I zipped past him and headed straight for my room. My heart thundered as I opened my desk drawer and pulled out the bracelet I had talked myself into and out of giving him since I made it. Leather, dark stones, wooden beads, and a pop of blue...warm, masculine, and inviting, just like Wyatt.

When I returned to the kitchen, I dropped it into his hand and then hopped back onto the counter before he had a chance to speak. "I know it's kind of silly," I said. "I don't even know if men wear bracelets." I shrugged, eyeing him as he studied the gift.

"You made this?"

I nodded. "You're always there when I need you. And I'm not always very good at saying thank you. I thought..." I dropped my eyes to my hands. "I thought maybe that would be a start. And the next time I forget to say thank you, you could look at it and know what you mean to me."

Wyatt crossed the room, the energy between us sizzling with each step. I wanted him closer at the same time I didn't want him anywhere near me because I didn't know what to do with the way my nerve endings sang at his approach. Or the way my stomach twisted. The way my heart rejoiced and my thighs tightened. I didn't know what to make of the low throb in my belly. I remembered the way he smelled and wanted to breathe him in, to wrap myself in his strong arms and sink into his strength.

"Thank you." Wyatt stopped in front of me, just out of reach. He slipped the bracelet onto his wrist, then stared at it for a long time. He had more to say, and by the look of him, I wasn't going to like it. "This will be the last time I see you," he finally said, his eyes lifting to capture mine.

My entire being rejected the statement. "What do you mean?"

"I can't live like my Dad. All this sneaking around is killing me. I bought myself a house and moved out of The Hut. Told Dad I would keep his secret, but I couldn't be involved in it anymore. I came here to say goodbye to you." He ran a finger along the beads at his wrist. "I didn't want you to wonder where I had gone."

Wyatt smiled weakly and panic rushed through me. I had just made room for him in my heart and now he was leaving. "Why?" I asked, anger chasing away any of the good feelings I had left. "Why even bother to say goodbye at all?"

"Because..." He shrugged, and his eyes spoke of so many things left unsaid between us. "You deserved to know where I went."

As much as I resented all of his preaching and soap-boxing, Wyatt had become the only stable part of my life. "I don't want you to leave." I huffed a sigh and gripped the edge of the counter.

"Keep my number." Wyatt leaned in close to meet my eyes, his hands on my knees. "I'll always be here for you if you need me. Always." His voice was heavy with emotion and his gaze flicked to my lips then right back to meet my own.

He leaned back and looked away, but in that instant, I realized that somewhere along the way, Wyatt had become interested in me. And, somehow, I had become interested in him. The thought of him distancing himself from my mom and me set my heart into a tailspin. I grabbed his shirt, pulled him close, my legs parting to allow room for his body, and pressed my lips to his.

I had been right about one thing. Today would be the day of my first kiss, but I had been wrong about so many other things.

It wouldn't be stolen from me; I would give it freely.

I wouldn't regret it; I would remember it forever.

It wouldn't be a thing of violence; it was a thing of beauty.

I wouldn't be disgusted and ravaged; feelings I'd never experienced before would bloom in my soul.

He made a sound I couldn't understand. A sound that did something to my body that both terrified and excited me. I tilted my head, parting my lips, making room for him nearer the aching throb between my thighs...

...and Wyatt pulled away.

"This can't happen," he said, though everything about his posture said his body didn't agree with his mouth.

"Why?"

He hesitated and I kissed him again, slipping my tongue tentatively out to meet his. He groaned and I melted, my face blushing as he put his hands on my shoulders and pushed me away. The warmth that had been growing inside me faded.

"Did I do something wrong?"

"What? God no. Everything about that was right."

He pressed his forehead to mine. "But that's why it's wrong. You're only seventeen. We can't—"

The front door swung open before Wyatt could finish. My mother froze in her tracks as she took in what was happening in her kitchen. Me, on the counter. Wyatt, nestled between my thighs, his hands beside my hips, caging me in. His frantic backwards step and the embarrassment on his face as he murmured his excuse to the floor.

Her knowing smirk told me everything. This day would be filed away in my mother's brain and saved for later use—right alongside all the other times she thought she had seen something happening between the two of us.

The only difference?

This time she didn't simply *think* she walked in on something happening between us. This time she *had* walked in on something happening between us.

Something I wanted.

Something I would never forget.

Something that might never happen again.

CHAPTER TWELVE

Wyatt

A year passed, and I expected Kara to fade into a faint hum in the back of my mind. I expected the space that had appeared for her in my heart to close up and make room for someone else. To heal like the wound it was. Perhaps there would be scars, but I could deal with that.

It didn't heal. I never stopped thinking about her. She was always there, a question without answers. She meant something to me, with all that barbed wire covering up her delicate soul.

At the end of each day, after closing up shop at The Hut and heading back to my house—a small, one-bedroom on the beach—I found myself wondering what had become of her. Her eighteenth birthday had come and gone. She was an adult now, and a high school graduate. Had she made good on her promise? Had she taken her money and set out on her own to forge her future out of nothing but hope and determination? Had she found her dream?

Or had she fallen into a spiral of self-destruction and mistakes?

Who had she become since the last time we were together?

I never forgot that kiss and spent more time than I wanted to admit wondering if it meant anything to her or if it was nothing more than an emotional reaction to what happened that day.

I hadn't heard from her since and I hoped that meant she had stopped finding herself in dangerous situations, though it was just as likely her pride had kept her from contacting me. That when things went bad, she had nowhere to turn, and so, all she could do was suffer the consequences.

It was late on a Friday night, with a spring storm rumbling in the distance when I finally heard from her. My phone pinged with a text and my stomach knotted when I saw her name.

I need you.

Three simple words that went straight to my heart. The thought of her needing me after all this time excited me as much as it scared me. I didn't hesitate to reply.

What's wrong? Where are you?

And then, her response...

Can I come to you?

I shot off my address and paced my small living room until I heard a car in my driveway, then the gentle thump of a door closing. I yanked open my front door as Kara raced up the walk and straight into my arms.

"What's wrong, sweet girl?"

The soft patter of raindrops started falling against the roof over my patio, releasing the smell of damp earth to mingle with the ever-present scent of the ocean and the sweet perfume of Kara's skin.

"She took it. She took it all." Her voice was thick with tears and I ran a hand through her hair. The year separating us didn't exist. I felt just as strongly for her as I did in her mother's kitchen. My desire to protect her flared to life and I tightened my grip, as if I could physically shield her from the pain I heard in her voice.

"Who took what?" I asked, though I assumed she was talking about Madeline.

Kara pulled back just enough to look me in the eyes. Light from inside my house spilled through the open door and illuminated her face. She had matured in the last year, the softness in her cheeks replaced by sharper angles that only further highlighted her shocking eyes. Her hair, still long and dark, now hung in gentle waves over her shoulders, and her lips, those delightful, full lips, were painted a dark red. Tears stained black by makeup trailed down her face.

Kara swallowed hard. "My mother stole all of my money. All of it. Every last cent that I had been saving since I was twelve." She choked back another onslaught of tears and stormed into my house in a swirl of pent-up emotion and lilac perfume.

I followed after, closing the door behind us, fully aware that she was even more beautiful in the light. She told me about the money she had hidden in a shoebox in the back of her closet, then finding the box, empty and open on her bed. "Did you confront her?"

"Of course I confronted her. And she denied the whole thing. She even had the balls to tell me she never touched the money in my bank account, even though I know she'd been helping herself for years!" Kara collapsed into a chair and dropped her head into her hands, her long hair forming a curtain between us.

"But why would she steal your money? Isn't my dad still supporting her?"

"He hasn't been as free with it, since you stopped helping him." She offered a weak smile and I saw zero judgement there, zero resentment. She knew why I had to step back from Dad and his craziness. She knew and she understood.

"What am I going to do?" Her question was born of sorrow. Of desolation. "That money has been my escape plan for the last six years. It wasn't enough that she stole my childhood. No. She had to steal my future, too. Now, I have nothing. I have to start over."

I crouched at her feet, my hands on her knees. "I am so sorry this happened to you." The words barely encompassed what I was feeling. I searched for something more appropriate to say, surprised to find I wanted to drive to Madeline's and confront her myself.

Kara's eyes met mine and they were softer than I remembered. Smarter. And jaded as hell. "It was stupid of me to think I could escape my mom."

"It's not too late to walk away from her."

"And how did that work with your dad?" Kara asked with all the fire I loved to hate about her. "Still show up for work every day?"

"I do," I replied, then explained how much better my life had become since distancing myself from him. How his mind games had less power over me and that I chose to keep my job at The Hut because I liked working for my family. I believed in my mother's dream for the place and fully intended to take over running the hotel when my dad passed. "Maybe there's a way you can create some space between you and Madeline," I finished.

Kara scoffed. "Experience would say otherwise."

"I'm not saying it won't be difficult. I *am* saying it will be worth it. And how many times have I seen you come back from some awful experience, stronger than ever? You can still open that jewelry store. This doesn't have to be the end of the dream. It's only the end of this road to it."

She shook her head, then fell silent as her gaze settled on mine. A slow smile lifted the corners of her lips. "It's good to see you, big guy."

I returned both the smile and the sentiment. "I'm sorry it's under such shitty circumstances."

"You and me both." She sat back and took in her surroundings as the rain fell in earnest, pattering against the roof and the windows.

I stood and took her hand, giving her a gentle tug. "Come with me," I said.

Kara looked at me, doubtful, but relented, allowing me to lead her through my house and onto the covered back patio. I leaned on the railing and invited her to do the same. "Take a deep breath," I said. "Close your eyes. Listen to the rain and the rush of the ocean. Feel the wind on your face. Breathe in the salt on the air."

Kara did as I instructed and I allowed myself the chance to study her profile. The wind blew her hair into her face and I brushed it away, then let my hand drop as desire surged through me. I wanted her more than ever and was fully aware that she was no longer a child.

"What can I do for you?" I asked, giving my attention to the rain instead of the hungry thoughts slipping through my mind. "What do you need?"

"When I found that shoebox, the first person I thought about calling was you. Not my best friend, even though she knows me better than anyone. Not the police, because it would be my word against hers. But you." Kara turned to me, her voice gentle, her posture exuding confusion. "Why? I haven't seen you in over a year and we hated each other more than we ever liked each other. So why, when my world fell to pieces, was the first person I thought about *you*?"

I wrapped an arm around her, intending to give her a quick hug and then pull away, but she melted into me, turning so her breasts pressed against my chest. "You were my first kiss," she said. "I thought it would be stolen by that awful man. Instead, I chose to give it to you."

"That's how it should be," I said. "We choose how much of ourselves we give away."

She dropped her chin. "Those are pretty words, but that's just not how it works. Everyone we meet takes what they can from us. Bit by bit. Piece by piece.

Each of us are scattered across our histories, held in the hands of those who saw something they needed and took for themselves."

Her words hit me. She would forever live in my heart, this girl I tried so hard to hate, bits and pieces of her life twined with mine. I would keep her there until the day I died. She would be mine to remember, to cherish, to despise. I had to wonder if she felt the loss of the things I kept.

"Do you think she feels bad?" Kara murmured against my shoulder. "Do you think even one little part of her regrets what she's done?" She looked up at me with such a painful mixture of emotion that I couldn't be immediately honest.

"Do you want the truth? Or do you want more pretty words?"

"I only want pretty words if they're the truth."

Thunder rolled across the water and the wind picked up around us. "Then no. I don't think your mom has thought twice about any of her actions. I think you are a pawn and she moves you around the chessboard of her life to maximize her own pleasure. Nothing she does is about you."

Kara tensed in my arms and pulled back to look at me. Her soulful eyes hit mine, then drifted to my lips. Her chest heaved—the soft swell of her breasts pressing into me—and she placed her open palms against my chest. I thought she was about to push me away. She didn't.

"That kiss? Our kiss? I've never had one like it since," she said, as if she had never changed topics in the first place. Her hands snaked up my shoulders, along my throat until she cupped my cheeks. "I haven't had many, but none of them compared to what I felt with you that day."

I grazed a finger along her lips and they parted as she gasped. A tiny sound, so feminine and filled with the need I felt for her that lust surged through my body.

"I haven't stopped thinking about you," Kara said, her eyes hot with adrenaline, excitement, desire. "I haven't stopped wanting you."

She closed her eyes and angled her face. As much as I knew I shouldn't kiss her, as much as I knew she wasn't for me, I crushed her lips with mine, gripping her back and drawing her close so my erection ground against her stomach. She moaned and parted her lips, rolling her hips against me, urging me on.

I threaded my fingers into her hair, so soft, so luxurious, everything I always thought it would be. She tasted of honeysuckle and I gripped her ass and lifted her to sit on the railing, just as she had sat on the counter the first time I kissed her. She wrapped her legs around my waist and pulled me closer, inviting me into the warmth between her thighs as rain drenched her back.

Her sweet gasps and moans made me hungry for more. I wanted to bury myself in her. To yank off her clothes. To fuck away the pain and confusion we had felt for each other over the years. I rolled my hips, the length of my cock pressing against her most sensitive parts.

If I was her first kiss, then I wanted to be her first lover. Her first love. I wanted to take all those firsts from her so I would be forever in her heart for the rest of her life, just like she would be forever in mine.

I palmed her pussy. "Has anyone been here before?"

She dropped her head back, moaning as she enjoyed the pressure of my hand. "No," she replied, so quietly the sound was almost swallowed by the rain.

Her admission dredged something up from deep inside me, the desire to have her mixed with the desire to protect her innocence.

"Take me, Wyatt." Kara met my gaze. "I want to give myself to you. You're the only one I've ever imagined giving myself to."

As much as my body rejoiced to hear those words, I felt myself pulling away. "Not like this."

Fear danced in those wonderful eyes. "Did I do

something wrong?" she asked, an echo of the same question from that day in her mother's kitchen.

"No. Not one damn thing." I ran a finger down her tear-stained face, rubbing at her streaked mascara with my thumb. "You're hurting. I can't take something so precious from you when you're hurting."

"It's mine to give," she replied full of the defiance I so admired in her.

"And you don't know what you're giving. I'll be one more person with a piece of you that you can never get back. And while I want to have it, believe me, I want you so bad it hurts." I took her hand and placed it on my erection. Her eyes went wide and her lips parted as she gripped my length through my jeans. "I don't want to take it under these circumstances. If you go home and calm down. If you wait a few days, until you've figured out what you're going to do about your mom. If, after you've gotten everything in order, you still want me, then you know where to find me. Until then, I can't. I just can't."

Kara's eyes flashed with anger as she hopped off the railing. "You could have just said no. You didn't have to wrap it all up in excuses to make me feel better. You don't like me. You never have." She ran her hands into her hair. "It was a mistake to come here."

She turned away and started to race inside, but I grabbed her wrist and pulled her close, kissing her with all I had to give. "It's killing me to let you go, but I'm not doing it for me. I will not be another mistake. I won't be the guy you look back on and regret."

Kara gazed at me, her eyes dancing across my face as she tried to make sense of what I was saying. Finally, she took a long breath and let it out slowly. Gave me her goodbyes, and left without saying anything else.

The next day, I kept my phone close, hoping to hear from her. I even started several texts of my own.

Hope you're feeling better...

Thinking of you...

Wish you hadn't left last night...

While they were all true, I didn't want to push her. If she came back to me, it needed to be something she wanted. Something she wouldn't regret as time passed. I would not be that guy she looked back on with remorse. I deleted my texts and waited for her to reach out.

She never did.

CHAPTER THIRTEEN

KARA

A month after my visit with Wyatt, I found an apartment and moved out of the condo, following his advice and putting as much time and space between my mother and me as possible. She and I still spoke, but it never went well. The more she realized she wouldn't get a rise out of me, the less I saw of her. That was fine with me. Eventually, I stopped reaching out altogether and my life finally started feeling like my own.

A year passed. Then another. Then two more.

Brooke and I went into business together, crafting and selling handmade jewelry out of a souvenir shop in a tourist trap strip mall. While the money wasn't always consistent, we enjoyed what we did, and somehow, that made up for the months when we had little more than Ramen and hope to survive.

While Wyatt swore he had rejected me the night Mom stole my money so he wouldn't take a piece of me with him, he had done so anyway. I thought of him often, mostly when I was working—my hands occupied, but my mind free to roam. That night four years ago was a favorite topic to come back to. What would have happened if we had slept together? Would it have been a one-time thing? The mistake he was so afraid we were making? Or would we have started a relationship that grew into something beautiful?

Up to that point, Wyatt knew me almost better than Brooke. He and I felt like kindred spirits, trapped by the choices of our parents, thrown together against our will. I often thought we would have eventually combusted, if had we gotten together. That we would have ruined each other. And so, while I resented him for rejecting me, I also recognized that he did us both a favor and saved us from the inevitable chaos we would have created together. After all, I didn't want him for money and he didn't want me for sex. If that was all men and women ever wanted from each other, where did that leave us?

Nothing good came from two people being in love. Nothing. I wasn't even completely sure love existed. According to the internet, there was nothing more pure than a mother's love for her child, and yet, I couldn't be sure I had ever felt anything but resentment from Madeline.

My friendship with Brooke was the closest thing I ever had to a committed relationship. I trusted her and she trusted me. I gave her my deepest secrets and knew she would handle them with care. Over the years, she had encouraged me to reach out to Wyatt, to see if there was anything there. She swore there was more to love than sex and money, that he had been in the right to turn me away, and that I had been crazy not to go back.

"Of all the bad decisions you ever made," she often said, "that was the worst."

A knock at the door startled me out of my thoughts and I glanced at the time. At a quarter till eleven on a Friday night, I couldn't think of a single positive reason for someone to show up unannounced, banging on my front door like he thought he could break it down. I grabbed my phone, ready to hit the emergency services button if things got bad, then crossed the room and peered through the peephole. What I saw on the other side set my heart pounding and my stomach dropping to my feet.

Wyatt leaned on the doorframe, his head resting against his arm. I cracked the door and peeked through, shocked to find him with at least a day's worth of stubble, red-rimmed eyes, and a bottle of whisky clutched in his hand. "What are you doing here?" I asked, when what I wanted to say was, are you okay? How can I help? What do you need? I'm so glad to see you. I've missed you so much.

His blurry eyes struggled to focus on mine. "Kara," he whispered. My name on his lips felt like a prayer.

I opened the door the rest of the way and he stumbled through. I steadied him as best I could and led him across the living room. He dropped onto the couch, looking surprised as he landed.

"How did you know where I lived?"

"Your mom." He lifted the bottle and stared at the contents, furrowing his brow before he threw back another swig.

"Hey, big guy." I perched on the edge of my coffee table and pried the bottle out of his hands. "Why don't you give that to me?"

He relinquished the alcohol without a fight. "My brother died." His words were so slurred, I wasn't sure I heard them right.

"What? Who?" That would explain the wreck of a man in front of me. Wyatt loved his family unconditionally. In my quiet moments, I had wondered how it would feel to have that love aimed at me. If someone he loved had died, I was sure it felt like part of him was dead, too.

Wyatt met my eyes, his pale blues swimming in despair. "Lucas. He died and they brought him back, but they're not so sure he's going to stick around much longer." His voice cracked on his last words, so coarse, so crude, his pain on display.

I listened as he struggled to explain. From what I could decipher, there was an attack on a military base in Afghanistan and Wyatt's older brother was caught in the carnage. He now fought for his life in a hospital overseas. Their mom had flown out to see him, but the rest of the family had to wait until Lucas was stateside and the wait was destroying Wyatt.

"I'm so sorry," I said, dropping down in front of him and searching out his gaze. "But, hey. Listen. Look at me. Right now, in this moment, Lucas is alive, right?"

Wyatt bobbed his head, then squeezed his eyes shut. "Last I checked."

"The past and the future only exist in our mind. You're not doing anyone any good by worrying about what *might* happen. Right now. In this moment. Your brother is alive. Focus on that."

Wyatt had never looked so broken. In all the years and all the different situations I had known him, I had seen him angry. Frustrated. Confused. I had seen him torn between his morals and his father's will. I had seen him fight himself in regard to me. But I had never seen him unable to process thought. I had never seen him helpless.

He dropped his head back and stared at the ceiling. "He was dead for two minutes," he said before he lifted his head and stared at me. "And I was dead for four fucking years."

His last statement caught me off guard. "What?"

"Why didn't you come back to me after that night?" Wyatt's gaze ignited with indignation. "I waited. I was sure you would come back. I let you go because I wanted to be respectful, and you just fucking disappeared." His voice rose as he finished his sentence and for a terrible flash of a second, I regretted letting him in.

"Wyatt." I stood, putting distance between us. "You're drunk."

"So? How many times have you come to me? Stuck and needing help? I was always there for you, Kara."

"And I'm here now." He was changing topics so quickly, I could barely keep up, his emotions oscillating between fury and pain. "And I'm going to make you a cup of coffee."

"I don't need coffee." He scooted to the edge of the couch cushion and glared at me. "I need you."

"No. You don't. The two of us together is a mistake," I said, repeating the mantra I used on myself when I got lost wondering what might have been. I disengaged and headed into the kitchen, pouring him a glass of water before getting the coffee out of the cupboard. His watchful eyes tracked my movements.

"How are we a mistake?" he asked as I handed him the water.

"How are we *not* a mistake?"

Wyatt set the glass down on the table. "You're the only person who knows me. You know my secrets. All the worst parts of who I am."

"And that's supposed to mean we'd be good together?"

"No. Or yes. Or maybe. You know the worst of me, but you still love me."

"I've never loved you." I dropped my gaze, hating myself for the lie. What I felt for Wyatt was complicated and now, when he was drunk and afraid for his brother's life, was not the time to try and untangle it all.

"You have. The same way I loved you. I can see it. Right now. It's in the way you look at me."

"That's enough of this nonsense."

"You see all of me."

"I see a man who is drunk and hurting and looking for things that aren't there."

The hisses and burps of the coffee maker interrupted me and I turned away from him, unable to watch the devastation in his eyes. I didn't know if what I saw was because of me or his brother and I needed him to sober up and talk to me rationally. I thought I had gotten Wyatt out of my system over the last four years. I couldn't have been more wrong.

With him here, all the pretty stories I had told myself about what we were disintegrated and I wanted him just as badly as I had that night in the rain. That night he had rejected me and I had, in turn, rejected him. Only, I never gave my virginity to anyone else. Not because I was saving it for Wyatt, but because his words stuck with me.

Whoever took my virginity would get a piece of me I could never get back. Every time I got close with someone—which wasn't all that often—I would look at the guy and wonder if he was worth that piece. Would he honor it? Would he cherish it? Would it be worth looking back on the moment and seeing *him*? Each and every time, the answer was no.

The only person who was ever worth that memory was Wyatt. And here he was, drunk and hurting and for the first time I understood why he rejected me that night. Something that special shouldn't be given without thought, as an anesthetic. If it mattered, then it needed to matter.

"I'm drowning, Kara." Wyatt dropped his head to his hands. "I'm drowning and I need you to save me. I need you to make it hurt less. I need you to help it all make sense."

I swallowed hard as I poured him a cup of coffee and set it on the table next to his water. "Drink the water," I said, avoiding eye contact. "The coffee, too if you need it, but the water first. You can sleep on the couch, and we'll talk in the morning when you're feeling better." I dropped a hand on his shoulder and he leaned into my touch before I pulled away to sit down next to him. We curled into each other and Wyatt fell asleep quickly. Somewhere along the way, I fell asleep too.

When I woke up the next morning, Wyatt was gone.

II

NOW

CHAPTER FOURTEEN

Wyatt

My father passed away in his office chair, an empty bottle of whisky in front of him. After decades of trying, the bastard finally managed to drink himself to death. A day later, I sat at his desk, amid a slew of papers, calling each of my siblings to deliver the news. I called Lucas last. As the oldest of us, he had the most memories of Dad before the alcohol stole the best parts of him. I suspected he would take the news the hardest.

"Hit me with the good stuff, Wy-guy," my brother said as he answered the phone.

"I have good stuff, and I have bad stuff. Whatcha want first?"

There was a pause and then, "Let's get the bad stuff out of the way."

"Alright. Bad stuff it is." I steeled myself to deliver the news. "Dad passed away last night."

And so, there it was.

I had been waiting years to say those words. For the entirety of my adult life, really. Knowing he was gone felt like a weight had been lifted from my shoulders. Like I could finally take a full breath. Like I could stop pretending to be the happy version of myself that everyone knew and actually just *be happy*.

"And the good stuff?" my brother asked, his voice nearly robotic in the total lack of emotion.

I huffed into the phone. "Dad passed away last night."

I imagined Lucas bobbing his head in agreement... understanding...acceptance. The asshole had held on too long as it was. "How's Mom?" he asked.

"You know Mom. She's taking it gracefully. Mourning the loss of the man she fell in love with while celebrating the loss of the man she ended up with."

I explained the funeral arrangements, which would be a massive public affair to celebrate the philanthropical side of our father the rest of the community knew. "Mom's calling in the cavalry," I said, when Lucas stayed silent on the other end. "It's time to circle the wagons, brother."

"I expected as much."

Neither of us knew what to say, but after what happened to him in Afghanistan last year, I found myself trying to prolong our conversations. "I didn't know whether or not to count all of us being together again as good or bad," I said.

"It's probably a little of both," came the reply. "Everyone coming?"

"Far as I know." I coughed and straightened a stack of papers. "Flights are being planned. Armor is being donned. Lines are being drawn."

"You make it sound like getting ready for war."

"Isn't that what happens when all of us come home?" I leaned back in my chair and closed my eyes. Living with Dad had nearly destroyed our family. Now that he was gone, it would be nice if we could heal. Before I could speak, Lucas said as much and I laughed at how our thoughts were following the same path, then agreed.

"Mom has rooms set aside at the resort, by the way," I explained. "You just need to get your bionic ass down here and it'll be like old times."

"My bionic ass, huh?"

"You've got so much metal in that backside, you might as well be Robocop." Teasing Lucas about his injuries was my attempt to keep him focused on the present. If he allowed himself to wallow over the loss of his military life, I was afraid he would slide backwards. And while he had come so far, he still had so much healing to do. I genuinely hoped he would find what he needed here at The Hut.

We ended the call and I steeled myself yet again. There was one more person who had to hear about Dad's death. Fighting the onslaught of emotions that arose every time I thought of her, I pulled up Kara's contact information and made the call.

Of all of us, she took the information the hardest. She gasped, choking on tears, questions falling past her lips in whatever order they came to her. In his way, Dad had loved Kara and she, in turn, had loved him back.

Kara

I set my phone down and stared at it for a long time before I called Mom. Wyatt hadn't been able to offer much in the way of consolation. His relief over Burke's death was evident even though he tried to hide it out of respect for my grief. I didn't expect the conversation with Mom to be much easier and I was right. When it came to grieving for the only father-type figure I ever had, I was on my own.

Mom answered my call with a heavy dose of annoyance, even though we hadn't spoken in months. Choking back my sadness, I explained what happened and the first thing she asked was, "What about the money?" Followed closely by, "Is there a will? Am I in it?"

I told her what I knew, there was a will, we weren't in it, and the money was now Wyatt's responsibility. She chastised me for not sealing the deal on our relationship years ago then hung up without even asking about the funeral.

When the day came, Mom backed out. She said it was because we would stick out like sore thumbs and she didn't want to risk people asking questions. A pathetic excuse, but she got points for consistency. There would be more than enough people at the funeral and we would blend in without raising eyebrows, but it was raining and she had a new boyfriend with deep pockets.

And so, I went by myself. I stood in the back, hiding my tears behind large sunglasses and a black umbrella. I watched the Huttons with their dry eyes and stoic faces, wondering if they had memories of

Burke they cherished, or if they were simply happy to see him go.

Of all the men in my life, he had been around the longest. I wasn't sure my own father—a man with no name, no face, nothing—even knew I existed. Burke was all I had in that department and as flawed as he was, I loved him very much.

As the service drew to a close, my gaze fell on Wyatt. Almost as if he could sense my eyes on him, he looked up, a sad smile tugging at his lips. As people left, I made my way to him. He opened his arms and I sagged into his embrace, wishing I could stay there for the rest of the day. He felt like comfort. Like safety. Like home. But after only a few seconds, he pulled away, offering me a shy smile.

We exchanged pleasantries. He asked about my life and I asked about his. For all that we were to each other, the superficial conversation only deepened my sadness. As far as his family knew, we were little more than strangers and my grief—which so obviously outweighed theirs—seemed out of place.

"I think you were the only person who still loved him," Wyatt said.

I swallowed hard, looking for an answer, when a beautiful blonde joined us. For one dreadful second, I thought she was Wyatt's girlfriend. Or wife. But the resemblance between them was strong, and I sighed in relief as I realized I was finally meeting Harlow.

"How did you know my father?" she asked and I was glad to have the sunglasses covering my wide eyes.

How did I know your father? He always said I was the daughter he wished he had. He compared me to you frequently and always found you lacking. Shame ran through me and Wyatt stepped in to save me once again.

"Kara benefited a lot from Dad's generosity."

The answer pacified Harlow's curiosity. Undoubtedly, she assumed I was connected to one of Burke's many charities. Wyatt politely finished our conversation as if I was little more than a stranger, then walked away with his sister, leaving me to deal with my grief alone. It felt like I lost two people that day. Two of the most important men in my life. Burke, and then Wyatt. Brooke had been right. Staying out of Wyatt's life had been a mistake. Wiping my eyes as I trudged up a hill toward my car, I found myself wondering if it was too late for us. The only thing I knew for sure was that I had to find out.

CHAPTER FIFTEEN

WYATT

Since Dad's death, my siblings had been staying at The Hut. Mom hoped they would each find a way to contribute and then move home so her family could be whole again, working toward the unified goal of running the family business. The only one who had found anything resembling work was Lucas, and the work he found—helping with the accounting and paperwork—made me extremely nervous. I hadn't had an opportunity to look through the last several years of bookwork, and didn't know what kind of mess Dad left behind. The rest of them did little more than disrupt my routines, though I could admit I was just as pleased to have everyone home as Mom.

That particular morning, I had an interview lined up for a new masseuse, but Caleb caught me in the kitchen. After listening to one of his fishing stories for as long as I could, I finally untangled myself and hurried toward the office to find a cute redhead staring into the room where Lucas sat behind the desk.

"You must be Catherine." I grinned as the woman turned, because there was no denying her attraction to my brother. "I'm Wyatt Hutton. That there is my older brother Lucas." I jerked my chin his way as I offered her my hand.

"Please," she said, swallowing hard as she glanced back into the office. "Call me Cat."

I nodded, doing my best not to laugh at how obviously flustered she was. I could only guess she had a thing for brooding Marines. "Cat it is. Normally I do my interviews in the office, but Lucas is busy doing..." I leaned through the doorway and stared at my brother. "Just what are you doing in there again?"

He leaned back and folded his hands behind his head. "Pretty sure I'm doing your job, aren't I?" He cocked an eyebrow and I laughed.

"Only because I couldn't trust you with Cat, here." I gave my attention back to her. "You and I can talk in the other room so the big bad wolf can finish pretending to do my job."

Lucas rolled his eyes at me, then gave the poor

woman his full attention again. "It's a pleasure to meet you," he growled in that overly intense way of his.

I led Cat into the sitting room and started the interview while bits and pieces of guitar music floated through the air, courtesy of Harlow. Cat took it in stride, and as she answered each of my questions, I realized how much I liked her. She would be a good fit here, though her obvious attraction to my older brother could be a potential problem.

"Wyatt?" Lucas stepped into the room. "Mom needs you in the office," he said, and my stomach dropped at the look on his face. Whatever Mom needed to talk to me about wasn't good, and my instincts swore it had something to do with Kara and Madeline—but I smiled as he offered to finish the interview.

"All that's left is the tour." I stood, suppressing another urge to laugh at Cat's expression. As cute as she was, she did *not* have a poker face. "I suppose even you could handle that," I said to Lucas, then paused on my way out. "Anything I should know about?" I whispered.

He dipped his chin and lowered his voice. "I found one hell of an accounting error. Or string of errors, really. Stretching back years. Either Dad's brain was more pickled than we realized, or he was into some shady shit."

I thanked Lucas and headed toward the office, grateful that he was more interested in Cat than he was in my reaction. If he had been paying attention at all, he would have noticed something was up. My poker face wasn't all that great either.

Thankfully, Mom was just as distracted. As she marched out years of accounting errors, some of them created by me and all of them leading back to Madeline and Kara, nausea churned and boiled. When Dad passed, I thought I was done with all this. I thought the stress would fade, the lies would end, and all his poison would finally bleed out of the family.

I had assumed I would be the only one to go through the books. I hadn't taken Lucas and my other siblings into consideration and I was in no way prepared to lie to their faces. As the day wore on, it became more and more obvious that no one suspected foul play. For the first time since he picked up the bottle, Dad's drinking was working in my favor.

Mom hung her head, lamenting her late husband's sickness, cursing him for reaching out of the grave to wreak continued havoc on our lives. I promised I would take over the job of getting things back to rights, helped her out of the office, then swore under my breath at the need for the continued deceptions. This part of my life was supposed to be over.

Was it right to cover things up one last time so the

rest of my family never knew the truth? Or should I explain everything because they deserved to know? I was stuck between shades of gray and couldn't see which of the two paths was right.

As soon as Mom was out of earshot, I called Madeline to let her know she wasn't getting one more cent from us. She spewed threats and bitterness, but I didn't listen. Relieved, I hung up and stared out the window, wondering how in the world I was going to explain my way out of that mess until Lucas came back to tell me about the interview with Cat. He seemed just as smitten with her as she was with him. His smile was a bright moment in a dark day and I focused on that instead of all the shades of gray.

CHAPTER SIXTEEN

WYATT

Sleep eluded me. For as much as I tried to steer my family away from the accounting errors, they kept asking questions, kept offering suggestions. They only wanted to help, but time and again, I found myself facing the decision of having to continue lying or just finally admitting what Dad had done. More and more, it seemed like the only way I could get my life back together would be if I sat my family down and explained everything—starting from the day he called me into his office and ending with the truth about what Lucas found in the books.

They would hate me when the story finally came out.

And they would have every right.

The problem was, the time for honesty was long past. I should have gone straight to Mom when Dad told me about Madeline. All this time later, with her husband gone, *I* was the man with the secret. *I* was the one who would take the brunt of my family's anger. After eroding my own morals and sense of self, I would be the one they pushed out.

Six months marched by, with that awareness coloring every moment. My family grew stronger and more stable while I learned to live on less and less sleep. Lucas fell in love and got engaged. Caleb and Eli stuck around long enough to know things were okay before they went back to their lives outside The Hut. Harlow settled in, growing closer and closer to Mom. And I drove myself insane, trying to protect everyone from Dad's final gift.

The one bright point in my life was that after years of silence, Kara and I now spoke often, mostly through text. I cheered her on as she continued to distance herself from her mom and she quietly supported me through my confusion.

I often laughed at how much I used to resent her in my life, because at this point, I couldn't imagine her not being a part of it. For as much as I supported her throughout her teenaged years, she was a rock for me now, listening as I needed to vent and offering hilarious GIFs in response.

A soft knock caught my attention and I smiled. It was just past dinner time, and I knew, I *knew* I would find Kara standing on my porch when I opened my door. Bracing myself for whatever madness she had for me that evening—after all, that was all we ever did, run to each other when our world was falling to pieces—I opened the door and found her there, a sad smile pulling at her lips.

"Hey there, big guy." She brandished a large pizza box. "I come bearing gifts." She didn't apologize for showing up unannounced. Nor did she apologize for making the assumption that I would be alone, she simply stepped inside, put the pizza on the coffee table, and pulled out a slice as she took a seat on the couch.

"Come on in," I said as I shut the door. "Make yourself at home."

Kara bit into the pizza. "Thank you," she said around a mouthful of cheese and grease. "I figured, you know, if I'm going to show up at your door with craziness, the least I could do is feed you."

I plopped beside her and helped myself to a slice. "Alright," I said. "Lay this craziness on me."

I listened, the pizza turning to sawdust in my mouth as Kara explained Madeline's growing discontent with the sudden loss of my dad's money. Kara sighed and tucked her legs up underneath her, her thigh pressing against mine. I expected her to shift out of the way and break the contact, but she didn't.

"I'm afraid she's working up her nerve to say something awful." Kara glanced at me, carefully gauging my reaction.

"How awful?"

"Pretty awful." She threw me an apologetic smile. "I'm afraid she'll call you and threaten to go to your mom and tell her everything if you don't start paying her again."

My jaw dropped. "But it's been six months. Why now?" I knew Madeline was unethical. I knew she was a parasite. I don't know why I was surprised to learn she was going to flex those muscles, regardless of how much time passed.

Kara shifted, her leg pressing even more firmly against mine. "We hadn't spoken since before the funeral, now all of the sudden she's reaching out, like I never kicked her out of my life in the first place, which is what clued me into the fact that she's probably gearing up for something. She had her claws in this other guy, but he isn't as free with the money as Burke was. At first she thought she just needed time. You know, it's easier to get into most men's pants than it is their wallets. But I think she's getting impatient."

I dropped my half-eaten piece of pizza next to hers

and glared at the wall. "I guess this is the push I needed. I have to be the one to tell them the truth. It can't come from your mom."

Kara grimaced. "How will they take it?"

"How would you take it if you found out someone you trusted had been lying to you for seven years?"

"I'd feel pretty betrayed."

"Yeah. Me too." I ran a hand through my hair and as I came to a decision about what I had to do, a sense of peace settled over me.

I would tell them tomorrow. And it would be hard. It would be more than hard. It would be fucking odious. But it would be the first step in making every-thing right and I was so ready to be done with all things Burke Hutton.

CHAPTER SEVENTEEN

Kara

Burke's death had been hard on me, but it was killing Wyatt. Dark circles stood out under his eyes. His mouth was a grim line. He had lost weight. His father's secret was eating him from the inside out. I hated knowing that part of what hurt him so much was me. My mere existence was a complication and I wished we had a better truth. Silence settled between us and I tolerated it for as long as I could before speaking up.

"Your brother looked good at the funeral," I said, searching out lighter topics, only belatedly realizing how sad it was that Lucas' almost-death counted as a lighter topic. "Seems like he's healing."

Wyatt smiled, though the light of it petered out

somewhere near his cheekbones. "He's getting married."

I grimaced, shifting a little, enjoying the feel of my thigh resting against his. "Ugh. No thank you. Marriage is not for me, you know?"

He didn't reply and I searched my brain for another topic, something, *anything* to keep him talking. I looked up to find him staring at me, his smile finally extending all the way to light up his eyes.

"Why do you do that?" he asked.

"Do what?"

"You can't stand to let things be quiet. You're always looking for something else to say."

It touched me that he knew me so well. Maybe that was the reason I decided to answer honestly. "I used to think it was because I couldn't stand silence." I shifted again, creating more contact between us. "But then I realized I could sit quietly with Brooke. With my mom. With just about anyone else. After some soul searching, I realized it was because I loved the sound of your voice. Still do."

Wyatt studied me and something in his eyes urged me to keep talking.

"And," I continued, even though I could feel heat rising in my cheeks, "I love the way it feels when I have your attention." I dropped my gaze, then lifted it to meet his again. "Why do you think I'm here? I could have just called or texted to tell you all of this. Lord knows it would have been easier. Instead, I'm drawn to you like a moth to a flame. You could so easily destroy me, but I don't care."

Wyatt widened his eyes. "Me destroy you? You're the one with the power here. Just one word from you or your mother and my life falls to pieces." Anxiety threaded his voice, tightening his throat. I hated what we were to each other, even as I lapped up his company like a greedy puppy.

"That's not what I meant. It's not my life you have the power to destroy. It's me." I placed a hand on his knee and the gesture felt more intimate than if I had jumped into his lap and kissed him full on the lips. "I've wanted you. I saved myself for you."

I hadn't intended to be *that* honest and the admission hung heavy and awkward between us. The only reason I came here tonight was to alert Wyatt to my mother's restlessness, but being around him did something to me. Something that left me feeling raw and unguarded. With anyone else, I would rebel against those feelings. With him, it was addictive. It thrilled me, like my feet were at the edge of a cliff, my arms spread wide, wind whistling past my body...

I watched as Wyatt began to understand. "You're still a virgin?" His voice was hushed, his tone awed—a man standing in a cathedral, stunned by the beauty, humbled by the serenity. "Why are you telling me this?"

"You told me that I didn't understand the weight of my virginity. That whoever took it would have a piece of me I could never get back. Those words stuck with me and I realized that for someone like me, someone who wasn't interested in having a relationship or falling in love, someone who was tired of having bits and pieces of herself scattered amongst the people in my life, I couldn't take that advice lightly. So, I saved it for you."

Wyatt's eyes went wide in shocked surprise, then narrowed, sarcasm gleaming in his pale blues. "What if I don't want it?"

"Then I guess I'm doomed to a life of celibacy." I grinned, despite the worry crawling up my spine. For as easily as I made my admission, my heart raced and adrenaline sung through my veins. A rejection would break me and Wyatt looked exactly like he was gearing up for a rejection.

"Kara..."

"Don't say no, big guy. Just don't. We've danced around this for years and I'm tired of wondering." I slipped off the couch and kneeled in front of him. "Is this how you want me? On my knees and begging?"

Something feral swam in his eyes and my inner thighs throbbed and tensed. By his look, Wyatt was a fan of having me on my knees. He stood and took my hand without a word, leading me past the kitchen and into the single bedroom of his house.

As carefully as if I was made of glass, he lifted my shirt over my head, then stared down at my heaving chest. He cupped a breast, bending to kiss the sensitive flesh above the soft, white lace of my bra. The air between us crackled with restraint and nerves twisted in my belly.

Given I was twenty-two years old with access to the internet and a subscription to HBO, I had my fair share of knowledge about what to expect, but knowledge and experience existed on two different planes. None of my 'learning' could prepare me for the surge of feeling as Wyatt's hands traveled across my bare skin.

The chill of vulnerability crashing against the heat of desire.

Wyatt moved slowly, caressing my body with a tenderness that sent my pulse racing. He savored each taste and as much as I reveled in the sensation, I found myself growing impatient. After waiting so long, after all the tension building between us since my childhood, I was eager to finally know what he had to offer.

I reached for the button on his pants, fumbling with the stiff fabric, aching to have my hands around his cock.

"You're greedy," he murmured.

"Impatient," I replied.

Without another word, Wyatt lowered me to the bed, pausing to relieve me of the rest of my clothes. I drew my knees up to my chest, uncomfortable in my utter nakedness. "No fair."

"You hiding yourself like that? I agree. No fair at all."

"No. You're still dressed."

Wyatt pretended to consider my statement. "Tell you what, sweet girl. You can earn my nakedness." He grinned and my nerves began to recede. "For every command I give you that you follow without question, I'll remove one piece of clothing."

"What? No!" I was embarrassed just hearing his suggestion. The thought of complying made me feel like I might die inside.

Wyatt *tsked*, then folded his arms across his chest. "That's a shame. That could have counted as your first one." The hungry gleam in his eyes twisted into good humor and I realized that this was Wyatt. That I trusted him. That I could relax and play with him.

"Fine," I said. "Your wish is my command."

"That's my girl. Now. Spread your legs."

I bit my lip, surprised by how hard it was for me to follow such a simple request. While I wanted to play his game, a very large part of me rejected the idea.

Following orders, making myself vulnerable, neither of those things came naturally to me. By spreading my legs, not only would I provide him access to the most private part of my body, but I would be dropping my boundaries enough to acquiesce. I wasn't sure which was the hardest aspect to overcome.

Wyatt lifted one eyebrow and drummed his fingers against a bicep. Slowly, fighting every instinct I had, I leaned back on my hands and let my knees fall open. His gaze raked over my breasts, down my stomach, and landed right between my thighs. My core turned molten as his eyes darkened. Without a word, he gripped his shirt and yanked it over his head, exposing a muscular torso and trim waist.

I might learn to like this game, I thought as I drank him in.

"Touch yourself."

My eyes went to his as I licked a finger and circled it against my clit. Wyatt rewarded me by slowly drawing his belt from his pants and dropping it to the floor.

"More."

While the order wasn't all that specific, I knew what he wanted. I slipped a finger inside, my gaze locked on his, questioning.

Is this what you want, big guy?

Wyatt undid his pants and stepped out of them.

His erection strained through his boxer briefs and I gasped, my lips parting, eager for his next order. I wanted those boxers off. I wanted that dick in my hand. I wanted to know him, to give the most precious part of myself to him.

"Lay back."

Without hesitation, I complied and Wyatt hooked a thumb into the elastic waistband, then let that last article of clothing fall unceremoniously to the floor. He climbed onto the bed, spreading my legs with his knees. My breath quickened as he kissed me, bracing himself with one hand while the other dipped between us. I hissed as he slipped a finger between my folds, dropping my head back at the intrusion, so foreign, so intimate.

"I'm on the pill," I murmured before I lost the ability to think or form words. I didn't want him questioning or holding back. I wanted him to take me the way he wanted me.

Wyatt nodded, then licked his lips, positioning his tip right at my entrance. I moaned. "I'll go slow," he whispered. "Tell me if I hurt you."

There was pressure, and pain, and I was full, so full, in a way I couldn't understand. My muscles shifted and flexed around him and I was nothing but a trembling bundle of nerves.

Wyatt cursed against my neck. "You feel so fucking

good." His words rustled in my hair and he captured my earlobe between his teeth.

Slowly, carefully, he began to move, rocking and rolling his hips, a freight train building up speed as he stroked his length against me. I lost myself, awash in sensations I couldn't name, amazed as something...

powerful

coalesced inside me.

It seemed monumental. Life-changing. Life-*affirming*. It seemed bigger than I was, and I struggled to understand how I could contain it all. My back arched and my skin pebbled. Wyatt surged inside me and it was all so new. All so much. I squeezed my eyes shut against the onslaught of sensory input.

"Look at me, Kara."

His voice sent another wave of goosebumps down my spine, so I opened my eyes and fell into his pale blue gaze. Something unlocked inside me and pleasure melted my bones. My body quivered and I cried out as my soul soared somewhere high above. Wyatt smiled down at me, then quickened his pace, leaving me awash in the fireworks of my first real orgasm as he chased down his own. He finished with a groan, his body quivering. I wrapped my legs around his hips and used my heels to draw him even deeper inside.

"Was it worth waiting for?" he asked as he lowered himself beside me.

I pretended to struggle to make up my mind, then turned to him with a grin. "We should have done that sooner. I should have come back after that night on your porch. You should have come after me when I disappeared. I'm ashamed of myself for putting it off so long." I rolled over to meet his gaze and asked the most important question of them all. "When can we do it again?"

CHAPTER EIGHTEEN

WYATT

After all the years and all we had been through, there was something poetic about Kara and me coming together. While the idea of a long-term, committed relationship made me uncomfortable, if I looked at things honestly, she and I had been in one for the last seven years.

She meant something to me.

She meant *a lot* to me.

Of all the people in my life, Kara had the clearest picture of who I was. She knew the worst, and still stuck around. I didn't feel judged by her. Or like I had let her down. In fact, she and I shared a mutual respect. We knew what it was to be manipulated by a parent. We knew what it was to hold someone dear, only for them let us down, and because of that I stood by her side and she stood by mine.

We were kindred spirits and after resenting her place in my life for so long, it felt wonderful to put that resentment down. I could let her in. I didn't know what we would be to each other moving forward, but finally acknowledging we were *something* felt like the beginning of...

What?

A relationship?

I didn't really know and it didn't really matter because whatever it was, we were in it together. The thought put a smile on my face and some pep in my step as I built up my inner resolve for what I had to do when I got to The Hut. This was the day I would tell my mother the truth about my father. My nerves were on edge, but it felt good to finally have a course of action that aligned with my sense of morality.

I pulled into my parking spot in front of The Hut at the same time as Cat. "You're looking mighty happy today," she said as she hopped down from her red Jeep sans roof and doors.

Her statement caught me off-guard. Considering the task ahead of me, I should have been worried, or tense. Instead, a sense of freedom moved through me.

"You know what? I am happy. Feeling better than I have in a long time."

Cat lifted her hair off the back of her neck, smiling as a breeze cooled the sweat on her skin. "That's great to hear. Someone like you only deserves happy days."

I held the door for Cat who ducked under my arm with a murmured thank you, then found myself face to face with Harlow. "Good morning, little sister."

"Back atcha." She crinkled her nose, as she studied me. "You seem...better."

I nodded. If it was obvious to Cat, it had to be a blinking neon sign for Harlow. "I am better. Where's Mom?"

"In the office." My sister jerked her chin in that direction. "She's got company though."

"That's fine. I'll just poke my head in and let her know I need to talk to her when she's done."

Six months ago, before Dad passed, I would have paused in the doorway to gather my strength for the confrontation that was sure to follow. Six months ago, I would have had time to take in what was waiting for me in that room, to think about the situation in front of me, and carefully choose my reaction.

But with Dad gone, I was comfortable to barge right in.

I had no chance to understand the situation I found myself in before I was up to my neck in it.

No chance to choose how to respond.

From behind the desk, Mom gazed sorrowfully at me, her face twisted with emotion.

The woman perched in the seat across from her flicked bleached blonde hair over one shoulder and grinned.

No one spoke while I glared at Madeline, the parasite who had latched onto my family and had no intentions of letting go.

CHAPTER NINETEEN

WYATT

"What the hell are you doing here?" I asked the woman I never intended to see again.

Mom sat back in her chair, her breath whooshing past parted lips. "So it's true."

I hadn't expected today to be easy. I knew I was going to drop one hell of a bombshell on my family. But I had thought I would get to do it of my own accord. I assumed I would tell them about the affair. About the money. About Kara's fears regarding her mother...

Kara.

Something dark and hateful slithered into my head, and I whirled on Madeline, the terrible *something* coalescing into a betrayal of the worst kind. "Is this why she was at my house last night? Why she showed up out of the blue? To distract me while you swooped in to ruin the rest of my life? Was all of this a set up?"

Madeline furrowed her brow while my mom looked even more distraught. "She who?" When I did nothing but shake my head, Mom raised her voice. "She *who*, Wyatt?"

Panic. Fear. Pain.

I heard it all, trembling through her words.

With my gaze locked on Madeline's confused face, I answered, "Her daughter."

The admission floored my mother, who dropped her head into her hands and let out a long, wistful sigh. "Madeline's going to the press."

She didn't need to explain the consequences of that action. If any version of this story got out, we would be ruined. With our strong family values at the core of our marketing efforts, a story like this would devastate our brand—even though it wasn't true.

"About Dad?"

Mom lifted her head and barked a laugh. "Yes. About that. And also about you and the completely inappropriate sexual relationship you've had with her daughter since she was sixteen years old."

My jaw dropped as all the air in my lungs rushed out of me in one harsh breath. "That's bullshit."

Madeline rolled her eyes. "Said every child molester in the history of the world."

"I am not a child molester." My voice rose and I paced further into the room, aware of Cat, Harlow, and any number of guests who might be in earshot.

Madeline crossed her arms over her ample chest. "Did you or did you not sit outside my daughter's school in your car when she was just a girl?"

"No," I replied with force, only to remember something like that had happened. So long ago the memory might have been constructed of spider webs. "I mean, yes, that happened. Once. But I wasn't stalking—"

Madeline raised one too-perfect eyebrow. "Did you or did you not bring my completely inebriated daughter home from a party when she was sixteen and you were twenty-one, then spend a night in her room while I wasn't there?"

"Yes, but—"

"And then, after I caught you, you conveniently forgot something and had to go back upstairs. Presumably to threaten her into keeping quiet about what you did to her."

The memory of Madeline stumbling through the kitchen, even drunker than Kara had been, danced through my mind. The leer on her face. Her assumption that we had slept together and her insinuation that she had been encouraging Kara to do just that for some time.

"That's not how it happened and you know it."

"I know my innocent little girl was hungover for most of the weekend after that little visit. I also know that you showed up to celebrate her seventeenth birthday. And shortly after that, I walk in on the two of you making out in my kitchen. Her perched on the counter, so small and delicate, trapped by your size as you literally caged her in with your arms." Madeline even managed to make her voice crack with barely contained emotion.

"None of this is true." I turned to my mother. "You know I'm better than this." Rage tightened my fists, and I took a deep breath to begin my rebuttal, but Madeline's next words caught me off guard.

"Do you or do you not have carnal knowledge of my daughter?" A smile darted across her face. She knew she had me. I had given her all the ammunition she needed when I mentioned Kara had been at my house last night.

A smart man would have lied. Or turned away. Or started yelling. Anything to create a distraction while he figured out how to react.

I, however, let images of the night before parade through my mind and, in that instant, the truth was written all over my face. The trap had been set and I walked right into it.

Mom closed her eyes and let her breath rush past her lips. "Oh, Wyatt..." I watched her faith in me crumble. I expected more from this woman who taught me to believe that love could conquer anything. How could she *not* see the lies for what they were?

"I need you to stop jumping to conclusions before you've heard my side of the story," I said to Mom before I turned on Madeline. "What exactly do you want? Why are you doing this?"

"It's more about what I don't want. I don't want the money to stop." Madeline picked at her fingernails, looking casual enough that I knew she was about to deliver her killing blow. "And I want you to marry my daughter."

"What?!" Mom asked in shock. "If anything you just told me is true, why...*why*...would you want him to marry your daughter?"

"He took her innocence," Madeline replied as if this were sixteenth century England and I just cost her an impressive dowry.

I scowled. "Don't pretend like she ever meant anything to you."

Madeline dropped the 'concerned mother' act. I watched it fall off her as easily as she put it on. "I'm no idiot," she said. "It'll be easy to cut the money off from me. Wait a few months. Maybe a year. Come up with a strategy to combat the bad press so the news doesn't ruin your business. But!" Madeline held up a finger. "If Kara is part of your family, then we're set. There's no way the money will stop."

"That's the most ridiculous thing I've ever heard." I fought the urge to pound a fist into the desk.

Madeline nodded and I didn't like the look in her eyes. The only true thing she said today was that she wasn't an idiot. The woman had as much cunning as she did crazy.

"It does sound ridiculous, doesn't it?" she replied. "But that's the thing. I've had so many beautiful years to get to know you. You wanna know what I've learned about who you are, Wyatt Hutton?" She paused and I swore I recognized Dad's smile twisting across her face. "You always do the right thing when it comes to your family. Even if it's stupid."

My father's words fell from her lips with such ease, I flinched as I remembered the day he said the very same thing to me, in that very same room. I turned to Mom who only stared at me with such hurt, such confusion, such *anger*...

"I can tell you two have a lot to talk about." Madeline stood and smoothed her skirt before sauntering out of the office.

CHAPTER TWENTY

WYATT

Mom stared at me, nostrils flared, face white, eyes wide. "I have never felt so betrayed in my entire life."

I clutched the edge of the desk and returned the look. "With you believing anything that woman said about me, the feeling is mutual." I needed a chance to process everything that just happened, a chance for my emotions to simmer down so I could think clearly, but Mom was talking a mile a minute, and it was clear I wasn't going to get that chance. This conversation was happening, whether I was calm enough for it or not.

"I just can't make sense of it all," she finished.

"I promise I'll explain everything, but you have to understand that nothing Madeline Lockhart says or does can be trusted." Saying her name had Kara's hot on its heels in my mind and the same terrible thought from earlier wandered through.

What if Kara knew this plan from the start? What if all our interactions were designed to lead to this moment? What if the Lockharts had been playing five-dimensional chess and I hadn't even been aware of the board?

My rational side rejected the idea, but the voice of self-doubt whispered away as I explained everything to Mom. I watched her battle her emotions as she looked for something to say. I'd had years to get used to this idea while she only had minutes.

"Oh, son," she murmured, her voice an essay in pain. "Why didn't you tell me? I expected this kind of stuff from Burke, but not from you. Never from you." Disappointment flickered across her face. "And the girl? What's her name?"

"Kara."

Mom bobbed her head as she repeated the name, her lips curling in distaste. "What's she like?"

What was she like? I thought back through all of our interactions, all the little things that brought us together time and again. She was a phoenix, rising from the ashes every time her life burned down around her. Instead of crumbling under the weight of disappoint-ment, she found ways to pull herself up stronger than she had been before. She was ingenious and capable, the kind of woman who could plan to open a business from the time she was a child, lose all the money she intended to use for the venture, then find a way to do it anyway. A woman with an independent streak so wide she'd fail a thousand times, as long as it meant she was doing things on her own.

I smiled despite myself. "She's nothing like her mother."

Mom leaned back in her chair, fiddling with the ends of the red braid slung over her shoulder. "Up until today, I would have said the same thing about you and your dad." She glanced up, tears forming in her eyes. "Apparently," she began, then swallowed hard and swiped at her cheeks, "it's possible to hide huge facets of our personality from the people who love us the most."

"I'm not like Dad. Not even a little bit." Mom drawing that parallel reignited my anger. And from the looks of it, it reignited hers as well.

"Then why did you keep this secret from me?" she asked. "Because he told you to?" Accusation laced the question, as if the mere fact that I did what my father said was enough to lock me up and throw away the key.

"Because he got in my head. Jesus, Mom! You, of all people, know what he was like!"

"You have no right to raise your voice to me. Not

now." Her presence seemed to both shrink and grow as she tried to look strong enough to cover up how much she was crumbling on the inside.

"And you have no right to compare me to him." I took a breath to calm down and lowered myself into the chair across from her. "I admit, I made a bad decision. I should have told him to shove his secret up his ass. But he knew just what to say to mess with my head." I waited for a response, but none came. "All I can say is that I'm sorry," I said. "I should have told you."

Mom leaned back in her chair, gazing at her lap. "I'll contact the lawyers and see what it takes to hit Madeline with a slander or libel case. We can't do anything about the affair, because the story is true. But the girl?" Questions swam in my mother's eyes and I was afraid she would drown in them.

"None of what Madeline said about us is true. Kara and I...we're complicated. But nothing inappropriate happened between us while she was underage. I swear."

"And she would attest to that?"

"Of course she would," I replied with more certainty than I was feeling. Most of me believed what I said, but a small part, a terrible part trained by Burke Hutton kept whispering that Kara was as false as Madeline.

"Unless she's in league with her mother," Mom said, echoing my worst fears.

"Which she isn't."

"Again, I would have said the same thing about you until today."

The look in her eyes said she knew her words would hit a weak spot, so I lashed out for one of her own. "If you didn't want me to end up like him, why did you stay with him after things got bad?"

Mom stared at me as I waited for the answer I knew I would never get. "Go," she said. "Talk to the girl. See if you still believe her. I'll get the lawyers on the phone and see what I can do from here."

I stood and stormed out of the room, pushing past a devastated Harlow on my way to the door. She called my name, but I ignored her, my focus locked on one single person.

The girl who had spent years wrapping me around her little finger.

The woman who owned my heart.

The child of the bitch who threatened to ruin me.

Kara Lockhart.

CHAPTER TWENTY-ONE

KARA

I stepped out of my apartment and froze on the small slab of concrete the complex called a patio as my gaze fell on Wyatt, sitting in his parked car, staring directly at me. I smiled and lifted a hand, even as dread settled in my gut.

Something was wrong.

Something was terribly, horribly, awfully wrong.

He pushed open his car door and stood, closing it behind him without so much as a smile.

"I have the worst case of déjà vu right now," I said, testing the waters with a joke. "I mean, how many times have I come outside to find you stalking me from your car?"

Wyatt strode toward me and something in his posture had me backing up before I got control of myself. This was Wyatt, after all. I had nothing to be afraid of. Especially after last night...

He stopped directly in front of me, his jaw and fists clenched, his nostrils flaring, his shoulders tensed. I reached out to him and he stepped away.

"Did you know?" He spoke with force and shook with restraint.

"Did I know what? What's wrong, big guy?" From the looks of him? Everything.

Wyatt started pacing in front of me, a tight path of angry steps. "About your mother," he said, stopping long enough to shove his hands into his back pockets and stare up at the sky. "Please tell me you had nothing to do with what happened this morning."

I stepped back from the hurt in his voice. I knew he was going to talk to his mom, and I expected him to be upset, but this...*this*...it was too much. Something else had happened. "Hey. You're scaring me."

He resumed pacing. "I'm trying to stay calm right now because you deserve the benefit of the doubt, but damn it, Kara! This is one hell of a coincidence!" His voice echoed off the walls the apartment complex and out of the corner of my eyes, I saw my neighbor peeking through her window to get a glimpse of the drama unfolding on the sidewalk.

"Come inside, Wy. Come inside and tell me what happened."

From the way he glared at me, he must have considered telling me to fuck off, but thankfully, reason prevailed and Wyatt followed me into my apartment. He wouldn't sit. He wouldn't look at me. For a few terrible seconds, he wouldn't speak. When he finally did, I wished he hadn't.

He told me about getting to The Hut, intent on explaining to his mom everything that happened between our families, only to find my mother already sitting in the office. He told me how she twisted our interactions into something awful. How she demanded that he marry me. As he spoke, his anger grew, my mother's story doing exactly what she had crafted it to do, spinning his emotions out of control until he didn't know who or what to trust.

"My God..." I murmured. "I thought you knew me better than that."

He stopped pacing and looked at me with such disdain, I flinched.

"I thought I did, too."

"You do!" I let him see my exasperation. "Are you really telling me you believe my mother over me? Let me tell you something, big guy. That's not going to fly."

Wyatt crossed his arms over his chest. "You're telling me you showed up at my house last night, out of the blue, tricking me into sleeping with you the day before your mom drops this bomb, and I'm supposed to believe it's coincidence?"

Tricking him? *Tricking* him? The fact that he thought anything about last night had been contrived had me questioning whether or not he deserved the piece of me he now permanently carried.

"It *is* coincidence."

Wyatt raked trembling hands into his hair. "I want to believe you. I'm trying to believe you. But why, *why*, did you keep coming back? We'd go years without seeing each other, but you just kept showing back up in my life."

"Because you were my rock."

He whirled. "Or was I your *mark*."

"Damnit Wyatt! You were my *everything*. You *are* my everything. I swear, I had no idea Mom was planning something so..." Hideous. Terrible. Diabolical. Hateful. So many words offered to fill that space, and I finally settled on, "...wrong."

Wyatt was too angry to hear me. He paced and raged, hurt by the accusations, panicked by his mother's response. Just as he had allowed himself to feel vulnerable toward me, his whole world had turned upside down and I was at the center of the devastation. I understood his anger, but my own emotions were spinning out of control as he flung his words with such abandon.

No.

Not abandon.

He intended to hurt me and he did. My God, he did.

I dropped to my knees in front of him, a last-ditch effort to catch his attention. It worked, though the look on his face broke my heart.

"You've used my pity against me enough, don't you think?" he asked, his lips curling in disgust.

It was the disgust that did me in. Of all the people in my life, only two knew what it was like for me to be Madeline Lockhart's daughter. Brooke, who had been my best friend since high school and Wyatt. The fact that her lies had any power over him at all was a punch to the gut I might never recover from.

"Fuck you, Wyatt," I said glaring up at him. "Just... fuck you." Those were the only words I could find to encapsulate the sheer, sickening disappointment of the moment.

His eyes narrowed. "Seems to me, you already did that." He started to say something else, but bit back the words. Eyes closed, he let out a long sigh, then turned on his heel and stormed toward the door.

If I let him leave, I would lose him forever. I knew that

because I knew him. And for as angry as he was at me, as angry as I was at him for believing anything my mother had to say, I couldn't lose him. Not now. He carried so many pieces of me, I would never be whole again.

I lurched to my feet and caught his wrist. Wyatt whirled and for one terrible moment, I was afraid he would hit me, but no.

No.

He wasn't that kind of man.

We glared at each other, emotions sizzling the air between us, and then he crushed his lips to mine, his hand gripping the back of my head, holding me hostage even as he gave me what I wanted. I gripped his back, my fingernails digging into his shoulder as his cock dug into my belly.

The kiss turned savage. A war of lips and teeth. Of frustration and confusion. We had found something in each other only to lose it the very next day, and our hearts demanded we find it again. His trust in me was tainted. As was mine in him.

Our bodies became a battlefield, two sides fighting to reclaim something they weren't sure they could live without. Clothing dropped to the floor and Wyatt pressed me against the wall, capturing my wrists in his hand and pinning them above my head. He penetrated me without caution, without care, his thrusts needy and harsh, and I lifted my hips to his, just as needy.

Just as harsh. The wall dug into my spine and I caught his bottom lip between my teeth as he beat a punishing rhythm.

And then, something softened in his eyes. The heat of anger faded from his gaze and he released my hands. His pace sped, though somehow that, too was changed. My body clenched around his, the frustration seeping out of me as Wyatt finished. He pressed his forehead to mine, his gaze intent. Concerned. Confused.

Neither of us spoke, though there was so much that needed said. "Don't leave like this," I pleaded through a thickening throat. We were better than this. We had to be.

Wyatt's eyes softened and he cupped my cheek. "I'm not going anywhere. I couldn't survive without you." He pressed a hand to his heart. "You've always been here. Always."

I covered his hand with mine, as if I could reconnect with the piece of me he carried. "Tell me you believe me. That you know I wasn't manipulating you."

He thinks you're just like your mom, whispered the voice I thought I had banished so many years ago.

Wyatt pulled his shirt on, his hair standing out from his head, looking as wild and untamed as I felt. "I believe you," he said. "I know who you are. You're nothing like your mother and I know you wouldn't do this to me."

I blinked back my surprise as Wyatt leaned in for a kiss so tender my heart broke. He ran a hand through my hair, gentle and delicate now that the storm of his fury had passed. On one level, it felt like I was getting everything I had ever wanted. That I had been obsessed with Wyatt since before we first met and now, despite my mother's best efforts, we could finally be together.

But that's where things got messed up.

Despite my mother's best efforts...

My mom had been pushing me toward Wyatt from day one. And when she couldn't succeed in pushing me to him, she had resorted in pushing him toward me.

That was, after all, the only reason he came to my apartment today. One giant, calculated shove from my mom had set this whole encounter in motion. As Wyatt and I stood there, sizing each other up, I had to wonder what happened in his head as he fucked me against the wall. What had caused the change in his eyes?

Had he forgiven me?

Or had my mother finally won?

CHAPTER TWENTY-TWO

WYATT

I wanted every minute Kara and I ever spent together to be real, a slow-motion dance of trust and vulnerability. I wanted to know that Madeline was crazy, using her daughter in one more terrible plan to leech money and comfort out of people who had rightfully earned it. I wanted to believe Kara.

I just...

...couldn't.

Not quite. Doubt had snuck in and made itself comfortable in my heart, a heart that didn't trust easily in the first place. I found myself weighing each of her words, searching for a chink in her armor that might tell me once and for all if she was lying.

"So now what?" Kara asked as she ran her hands through her hair.

"That's a good question."

She stared at me, her eyes bouncing across my face, thoughts ticking away behind them. I watched her defensive walls come up around her. The hardening of her gaze. The lift of her chin. I had to wonder if I looked the same to her. If she could see me analyzing every move she made, every word she said. In that moment, I hated Madeline for all the damage she had ever done to Kara, as well as for the damage she had done to my family, and now, the damage she had done to us.

"Relationships were never really my thing." Kara painted a blasé expression across her face. "So yeah, this is all getting a little messy for me." Except I knew her well enough to see how much she regretted those words.

Confronting her would only make her dig her heels in, so I called her bluff. "Yeah. The two of us together seems out of the question now, given that neither of us can trust the other."

"I trust you." Judging by the defiance in her glare, Kara intended her statement to come across as a slap to my face. After all, I was the one who had come barging into her apartment, armed with accusations of treachery. But I caught the glimmer of doubt in her eyes.

"But do you really?" I asked. "You really trust me after all this?"

"Why wouldn't I?" Chin lifted. Fire in her eyes. God, she was beautiful.

"Because Madeline told me she wouldn't go to the press if I married you, and you know I would do anything to protect my family. So, I assume, there has to be part of you that wonders if I'm still standing here because I want to, or because I feel like I have to."

Kara dropped her gaze, her eyes flickering shut. "Why does it have to be so complicated?"

It was a great question. One I didn't have an answer to. "Would she do it? Would your mom go to the press? Make those accusations about me?" I choked on the word. It would be so easy to twist my relationship with Kara into something ugly.

"I don't know. I'll talk to her, Wy. I'll talk to her and beg her not to do it." The look in her eyes was so worried, so innocent, that I truly believed she had nothing to do with her mother's plan.

And that was a problem. If she was playing me, anything she said and everything she did could be part of the game.

"Would she listen?"

Kara's face fell. "Probably not. But if she does go to the press, I'll stand by your side and tell everyone the truth. I'll even talk to your family, if you think that would help."

It would take a leap of faith for us to trust each other. A lifetime of manipulation had our instincts screaming to cut our losses and run. I said as much, cupping her cheek. "But I'm not going to run away from you. I couldn't if I wanted to. Wherever I go, you're with me."

She leaned into my hand and closed her eyes. "I am so tired of being used by her."

"I know, sweet girl."

I wanted to tell her that this time would be different. That I would do everything I could to keep her safe. While the last part was true, I would fight for her just as fiercely as I would fight for my own family, I couldn't promise that she would come out of this unscathed. If her mother was willing to drag her daughter's name through the mud, then there was no telling how far she would go to get what she wanted.

And...if by some chance I discovered that Kara had been in on the plan after all, there would be no end to my wrath.

CHAPTER TWENTY-THREE

WYATT

I made an appointment to see my mom. I did it as a show of respect, calling to let her know I wanted to talk instead of showing up out of the blue. She sounded both relieved to hear from me and hesitant to see me and we ended the call without having much to say to each other. Kara and I drove to The Hut together and I groaned when I saw the parking lot. We wouldn't just be speaking to my mother that day. She had called in the cavalry and the entire family waited for me inside. That was what Huttons did, after all. When one of us needed help, we flocked together to provide support.

Regardless of what lay ahead, we would get through this. Of that, I had no doubt, because that was also what Huttons did. We stuck together. We moved forward. We overcame.

Kara gave me an encouraging smile as we took the steps to the front porch. "I've never been here," she said. "I used to stalk the pictures online, wondering what it would be like to truly be part of your family. I was so jealous of you all. Burke was the closest thing I ever had to a dad, as creepy as that sounds now that you and I are, you know, together." She trailed off as I pulled open the front door and ushered her back to the kitchen where I was certain my family would be waiting for me around the large oak dinner table.

My brothers glared as I stepped over the threshold, Caleb bolting out of his chair and cursing my name. "How could you?" he shouted as he lurched around the table. "How could you do this to us?"

Lucas caught his arm before Caleb could get to me. "Sit down." He used his Marine voice, barking the order with little room for disobedience. "Let Wyatt talk before you lose your shit."

Caleb did not sit down. He stood behind his childhood seat at our table, his knuckles white as he gripped the back of his chair. "I used to respect you so much. Lucas left. Dad was useless. But you stuck around and made sure the rest of us were okay. I looked up to you. And now I find you're no better than him... What the hell am I supposed to do with that?" He looked away, letting out a long breath as a vein in his temple pulsed.

My sister looked at me with sad eyes and my mother wouldn't look at me at all. All of them ignored Kara, as if refusing to acknowledge her presence would erase her from the family's history.

"You know," Lucas said as I sat. "I always wondered why you stayed. It never made sense to me. Never. I thought it was to protect them." He made a gesture, encompassing our brothers, sister, and mom. "You knew what Dad was capable of, just as much as I did. I thought you stayed to make sure they were all safe."

"That's exactly why I stayed," I replied, nodding.

"Bullshit!" Caleb spat the word. "You stayed to protect yourself."

I shook my head, meeting my family's gazes head on, digesting their hurt, their betrayal, their confusion and sadness. I deserved to see their pain, but I also deserved a chance to be heard. Carefully, I explained the day Dad called me into his office and shared his story.

I explained my revulsion, placing an apologetic hand on Kara's knee at the word. I explained my instant reaction, telling Dad to go to hell and refusing to keep his secret.

Eli ran a hand along the back of his neck. "And yet here we are."

"He said I would destroy the family if I told any of you." Dad spun a perfect web of lies and manipulation, capitalizing on my fears, my strengths, my weaknesses. He knew exactly what to say to make me do what he wanted, without question. I tried to explain how the time I spent with him was like playing chess. I would move and he would react, over and over until I was in too deep. "Every time I worked up the courage to tell him I was done, he managed to get me all tangled up again. You have no idea how hard this has been. How—"

"Don't even consider trying to make us feel sorry for you." Caleb turned his back, unable to even look at me.

"At least hear what he's trying to say before you judge him." Kara's clear voice rang out, shocking my family into silence.

"You don't get to speak here," my brother growled.

My mother held up a hand. "Enough, Caleb. Your brother made a mistake, but no one makes it through life without their fair share of those, and we all know what life was like with your father. Let the girl talk."

Kara lifted her chin and met my family's eyes. She didn't flinch from what she saw there, though I wouldn't blame her if she had. The day I met her outside Madeline's condo, I hated her. In my mind, she was as much at fault for what was happening as our parents, and I could see my brothers and sister coming to the same conclusion. They were wrong, of course, just like I had been.

"I've always been jealous of Wyatt's love for you," Kara said, her sultry voice low, but clear. "Every now and then, I would get a glimpse of what it must be like to have someone love you unconditionally, the way he loves you. He puts his needs aside to take care of yours, and he does it with a smile on his face and a heart free of resentment, so you probably have no idea how much it cost him..."

She outlined the sum of our history together, painting me as a selfless hero. Someone who was always there when she needed me, even when her mother wasn't. She explained the day I picked her up from jail, my dislike for her so very clear, yet my desire to protect her still making itself known as I couldn't help but try to keep her from repeating her mistakes.

She explained the night I rescued her from the party when no one else would. How I helped her out of that house and into the car, then held her hair while she threw up. She explained how many times she had texted her mother for help, but when she woke to find water and ibuprofen waiting for her, it had been me who left them. Not her. That she had spent weeks wondering what I wanted from her, because she hadn't had much experience with kindness that didn't come without strings attached.

She explained the day I showed up to tell our father to shove his secret up his ass. How she could tell then that he had me so tangled up and twisted that I couldn't see the path in front of me. She explained the day I saved her from her mother's boyfriend, the only reason I had shown up at all being that I had finally told Burke I was done, but didn't want to leave her without an explanation.

"Wyatt is a born protector," she said, "and that trait extended to include me, even though I never deserved it. Imagine what he's put himself through, trying to understand the best way to keep you safe from Burke. Was it better to keep the secret? Sheltering you from such a terrible truth? Are you better in any way now that you know, or would you have been happier if it had never seen the light of day? And now, he's even willing to shackle himself to me, if that's what it takes.

"He took one look at your face," she continued, dipping her head toward Mom. "He saw your fear over what might happen if my mother went to the press and decided that, as usual, he would do whatever it took to put things back to rights. Even if that means spending the rest of his life with someone he doesn't love."

Even as Kara claimed I didn't love her, I knew it

wasn't true. I had loved her for years. And listening to her talk to my family proved that she had, in turn, loved me as well. The realization couldn't have come at a worse time. I schooled my face into something I hoped no one could read, though one glance at Harlow proved she had seen what none of the others had.

"I'm sorry I hurt you," I said to them. "I'm sorry I've broken your trust in me, but I swear, I was trying to do the right thing."

Harlow nodded her understanding. "I know what it's like to have Dad's undivided attention. It's like you're drowning. Like up is down and good is bad. It sounds like he was doing that to you, and I'm sorry you had to endure it." Eli and Lucas nodded their agreement while Caleb sighed. I watched his anger seep out of him as he met my eyes.

"She's right," he said. "They both are. I lumped all of Dad's bullshit right onto you and it doesn't belong there. He was a twisted fuck, but you've always been there. For all of us. I am who I am because of you."

"That's not saying much," Eli joked, giving Caleb a playful smile. The whole family chuckled and their forgiveness wrapped around me. They knew who I was and how much they mattered to me, and they loved me just as much as I loved them.

Mom studied Kara for a long moment. "Will your

mother follow through on her threat? Will she go to the press with her accusations about my son?"

Kara dropped her chin. "She'll go through with it," she said, looking up. "Nothing gets between my mother and the things she wants."

Mom's eyes blazed with the ferocity I used to see when Caleb came home with a fat lip or Harlow spent days in hiding—the look of a mama bear stretching her claws. "She'll be in for a surprise, then, because nothing gets between me and my family."

CHAPTER TWENTY-FOUR

Wyatt

The conversation moved on to legal matters as Mom distilled what she learned from the lawyers. It became more and more clear that my brothers and sister hadn't come today with the sole purpose of confronting me. They showed up to hear the story, to understand, and to figure out how to move forward. I left the meeting feeling like I had my tribe at my back.

Kara and I drove back to my place in comfortable silence. She twined her fingers through mine and gave my hand a squeeze, before setting her attention out the window.

"Do you really believe all those things you said about me?" I asked as we pulled into the driveway.

Hearing her describe how she viewed my role in her life had been a beautiful thing. I wanted to wrap this woman up in my arms and hold her close, as if my proximity could erase all she had lived through.

"I saved my virginity for you, big guy. Of course I meant everything I said. But don't go getting a big head or anything," she replied with a grin.

"Wouldn't dream of it."

We climbed out of the car and made our way up the walk. The palm trees in my front yard rustled and the breeze blew the scent of her perfume my way. The sun shone from a brilliantly blue sky and a weight I had carried around my neck eased off my shoulders. Everything was going to be okay, and I had this amazing woman by my side. After dealing in the darkness cast by my father's shadow for so long, she was the light at the end of the tunnel.

I swept her into my arms and kissed her, parting her supple lips with my tongue. She pressed her body against mine and I felt whole as the pieces of each other that we carried came together. Her hands trailed up my back and I grabbed her ass.

"This is a thing of beauty," I said, giving it a squeeze. "Sheer perfection."

It dawned on me that we had never been out as a couple. Never had the luxury of walking the beach, hand in hand, or laughing over the music at a bar as we leaned in close to be heard. Our relationship had blossomed under the worst of circumstances, a flower shoving its way through cracked concrete in the city. Despite the environment, it kept growing, kept blooming, and now, it was a masterpiece of delicate strength.

"You wanna, I don't know, do something?" I asked, drinking in her beauty.

"I'd like to do you," she replied, a devilish look in her eyes as a blush crept into her cheeks.

I stared at this woman and saw all the years connecting us, tying together our hearts and minds in ways we hadn't fully recognized yet. I kissed her again, savoring the way her curves pressed softly against my body. "Sold," I murmured, my lips brushing hers.

She giggled and stepped out of my arms, then leaned on the side of the house while I slipped my keys into the lock.

"It's amazing how much Harlow looks like you," she said, gaze locked on something off in the distance, "considering she's your half-sister."

I choked back a laugh and gave Kara a funny look, but she continued without pausing.

"Mom said Burke always went on and on about how much he hated seeing another man's features in her face..." She trailed off as she took in my stunned expression.

I stopped fiddling with the key as all my attention

went into Kara's previous statement. Another man's features? Half-sister? "What the hell are you talking about?"

She sucked in her lips and her eyes went wide. "About Harlow. And your mom's affair..."

"My mom's affair? You're kidding, right?"

"Why would I joke about something like that?" Her jaw dropped. "Oh, shit. You didn't know..."

As Kara stammered out apologies and explanations, I thought back over Dad's disdain for Harlow and it all made a terrible kind of sense. I couldn't be sure, because my own memories were so foggy, but it seemed like right after Harlow was born, Dad's drinking got worse. If she was a daily reminder of infidelity, of course a man like that would make sure she knew she would never measure up. Burke Hutton could never see past the act, would never be able to forgive the innocent child who had nothing to do with her parents' choices.

Kara was still apologizing, but I couldn't find the brain power to talk to her.

...Mom had cheated on Dad...

...Harlow was the product of infidelity...

...Dad's alcoholism became a problem because of my mother...

...yet she was comfortable judging me for harboring

secrets when she had one bigger than anything I could imagine...

Did Harlow know?

Oh, poor, sweet Harlow...

"Wyatt?" Kara put her hand to my face and it was only then that I realized I was sitting on my porch in front of the door, staring at the peeling white paint on the wooden planks.

I let out a long sigh and shook my head, inviting her to sit beside me. "It feels like I'm losing everything," I said. "All of it. All at once."

"I really thought you knew." Kara curled into me, tucking her head against my shoulder.

"My family is nothing but secrets," I said, though I struggled to accept that Harlow wasn't Dad's. My mother wasn't that kind of woman. She smiled her way through hard days and fought for people who had less than she did. She was a paragon of goodness. Warm hugs that smelled like fresh bread and the kind of intelligence that could grow a business from the ground up. How could she be capable of something like this?

Kara leaned in to me and I wrapped an arm around her shoulder. "My whole world is upside down," I said. "But at least I have you."

A tiny corner of my subconscious pricked up and reminded me that I might not actually have her at all. That she, too, might be as false as all the other women in my life. I ignored it. I had to. All this manipulation was making me sick to my stomach and I needed the hard truth of Kara to pull me through.

For the first time, I understood why Dad chose to drink.

CHAPTER TWENTY-FIVE

Kara

The next couple days passed in a strange rhythm of work, time with Wyatt, and an ever-growing feeling of rage toward my mother. Considering I never took the time to explain everything Mom did to the Huttons, Brooke put up with my volatile moods like a champ. Though, judging by the way she had slammed around our jewelry store today, full of long sighs and frustrated glances, she had reached the end of her patience.

"Seems like something might be bothering you," I joked, after she banged a bag of clasps down on a table in the back, then cursed when they spilled and rolled all over the floor.

"Me?" she asked as she dropped down on all fours.

"*Me*? You think something is bothering me?" She peeked over the table and the incredulity on her face faded when she found me laughing. "You think you're so funny, don't you?"

I nodded my agreement. "Sure do."

Brooke stood, the errant clasps clutched in her fist. "Well, then, funny girl, yes, something is most definitely bothering me. Can you possibly guess what it might be?"

"Hmm…" I tapped the side of my chin with a finger. "Is it the awesome new bracelet I made yesterday? Maybe feeling a little jealous of my superior skill?"

"No…definitely not that."

"Is it the fact that it's almost lunchtime and we've had exactly zero customers?" Add that to the zero customers we had yesterday and things were starting to look grim. I would captain this ship until the very end, but lately it felt like water was creeping up around our necks.

"No. It's not that." Brooke rolled her eyes. "I mean, well, yes, that bothers me. A lot actually. But that's not the thing I'm talking about."

I gave my friend a smile and dropped the act. "Look, I'm sorry I've been so difficult the last few days."

"You've been just a touch more than difficult…"

"Fine. I'm sorry I've been..." I searched for the word that might encompass all I had been feeling since everything that happened with Wyatt and his family. Frustrated. Disappointed. Distraught. There was a rock buried in the pit of my stomach—cold and hard—and the sensation was spreading throughout my body. This all-pervasive sense of *something's wrong* and the harder I tried to shake free, the more it clung to me.

Things with Wyatt were good. For so long, we had been on different pages regarding what we were to each other. Finally, we could both agree that the chemistry between us was more than just attraction. More than just the natural side effect of being pushed together through the consequences of someone else's bad decisions.

And that felt good. Really good. So good, I fell asleep with a smile on my face and woke up still smiling. But that didn't stop me from worrying because no matter how happy we were together, that rock in my stomach wouldn't go away.

"Is it your mom?" Brooke asked, leaning across the table with kindness in her eyes.

"When isn't it my mom?" I explained the situation while she listened with jaw dropped and eyes wide.

"That's..." Brooke shook her head, as if to clear her thoughts. "How is this your life?"

"How can you even ask that question? You know my mom almost as well as I do."

Brooke frowned. "You need to talk to her. She has to stop doing this to you. Like yesterday."

"Believe me. If talking to her did any good, my life would have been significantly easier starting a long time ago. Come on, Brooke. You know this as well as I do. My mom doesn't see reality. She sees what she wants to see and warps everything so she's not at fault. If I told her to leave me alone..." I couldn't imagine a life where that actually happened, my mother keeping her fingers out of my affairs.

"What?" Brooke held out her hands. "What more could she possibly do to you?"

"Well, she wouldn't listen. I know that much for sure."

"But what if she did?"

I gave my friend a look. She knew the answer to that question and it was a waste of breath to even ask.

"Fine," she conceded. "She won't listen. But maybe you'd feel better. Maybe you could say all the shit that's eating you up from the inside out and could finally start to heal. And then cut that crazy woman out of your life for good."

Could I do it? Could I cut my mom out of my life? We barely had a relationship as it stood. The only reason I ever spoke to her was when she needed something or I felt a sense of guilt or obligation to her...

"I don't know, Brooke. What would I say?"

"What wouldn't you say? You could finally unleash all the ways her narcissistic ass has ruined your life. Start at the beginning, then walk her through it all, step by step until she finally gave you the apologies you deserve."

"Ha! Apology? Maybe you *don't* know her the way I thought you did."

"Okay, fine, she wouldn't listen *or* apologize. But what do you have to lose? The way I see it, the worst that could happen is that she might try and ruin your life. Oh wait...that's already happening." Brooke gave me a look.

"And the best?"

"Well, I wouldn't expect a heartfelt mother-daughter moment or anything, but maybe she would leave you alone and you could stop scaring away our customers by being so grumpy."

I bobbed my head as I considered her words. I had never stood up to my mother. I had stopped calling her. Stopped reacting to her craziness, but I had never actually told her how I felt about the way she treated me. The more I thought about it, the more I realized it would feel so damn good to say all the things I wanted to say over the years. I knew she wouldn't hear me. She would spin things around until I sounded crazy and she sounded like a victim, but maybe, *maybe* I could get it all off my chest and then close the door on her forever. Start a new chapter in my life. One that included Wyatt...

"Do you love him?" Brooke's question caught me off guard and made me wonder if she could read my mind.

"I do. I think I have for a long time."

"Does he love you?"

"I think so." I thought back to the kiss on his front porch, the way he looked at me as if I was the most beautiful thing he had ever seen. Wyatt was the best thing that ever happened to me and it was past time I stood up to my mom. She deserved to hear what I thought of her and Wyatt deserved to have me tell her exactly how awful she was being.

"I am by no means an expert on love, but if you've found it with someone, and if he's as decent as you've always made him seem, then you need to fight for him. You can't let your mom ruin the first good thing that ever happened to you."

"Second," I said, smiling.

Brooke tilted her head and scrunched up her nose. "What do you mean?"

"He's the second good thing that ever happened to

me. You are the first." I drew my friend in for a hug while her words danced through my mind.

She was right, of course.

Wyatt was worth standing up to my Mom.

He was worth fighting for.

He was worth putting my heart on the line because God only knew how many times he had put himself on the line for me.

CHAPTER TWENTY-SIX

WYATT

The second time I went to see my mom after Madeline's visit, I didn't call to make an appointment. I simply showed up—overflowing with accusations and questions—barged into the office, and sat down. Mom regarded me from Dad's chair, dwarfed by the size of the thing. Sun fell through the window, casting shadows across her face and I wondered which was winning, the darkness or the light. She greeted me with an edge to her voice, a feature that seemed to come with the chair. I took the seat across from her and returned the greeting.

"How are you?" she asked, searching my face as if she could read the answer in the set of my eyes and the curl of my lip. I recognized what she was doing because I had done it for years, trying to read my father's mood as we faced off across the desk.

There wasn't a good way to start this conversation, so I dove right in. "I know about Harlow."

Mom scrunched up her brows, tilting her head as her lips parted. "About Harlow? What do you mean, you know about Harlow?"

"I know she's not Dad's." Mom's eyebrows hit her hairline, but I held up my hands and continued. "And I'm not judging you. I'd have to be a certain kind of asshole to stand where I'm standing and look down at you for trying to cover up a mistake." I offered a weak smile.

"Harlow is your father's child." Mom dropped her head into her hands. "How in the world did you hear this?" A moment later, she looked up, guilt softening her eyes. "Did you hear it from him? Have you been holding on to this secret all this time as well?"

Her response wrapped a tight hand around my heart. "I heard it from Kara. Dad never said a word about it to me." A cloud covered the sun and darkness descended on the room. I fought the urge to turn and see if he was looming in the doorway. He was gone. He had been for months, but in this moment it still felt like he was everywhere.

"Why would Burke tell *her*? God, that man...I

should have left when things got bad. I could have saved Harlow from his spite. Caleb from his condescension. I could have saved you from having to deal with this giant mess." Mom trailed off, her eyes so unbelievably sad. "I can't imagine what you've been through. Of all my children, you have the biggest heart. To know he took advantage of it the way he did..."

Her grief unsettled me, but I needed to know the whole story. My father was the source of so much sickness in our family, but if the poison ran deeper, I needed to know. "What happened, Mom? What happened with Harlow?"

Love was a funny thing, sometimes beautiful, sometimes terrible. It blinded you to faults and smeared lines you thought were indelible. It brought out the best and worst of a person, oftentimes in the same moment. I watched Mom's love for her daughter boil to the surface, churning with whatever it was she felt for her husband. She placed both hands in her lap and let out a sigh.

"After Eli was born," she began, her voice low and thick, as if these words weren't meant to be spoken, "your dad and I struggled. With four children and a rapidly growing business, our plates were full and our relationship was suffering. We fought at first. Awful fights filled with dreadful things. When the rage boiled away, there was nothing left. We agreed to stay together for you boys, but to live as separately as we could, but Harlow happened anyway, and your father refused to believe she was his. I had been working closely with one of the contractors and Burke swore I was sleeping with him. Somehow, it was easier for him to believe I cheated than to look at that little girl and see all the ways she looked just like him. All he saw was white-blonde hair and pale blue eyes, so much like the rest of you, except in her it was treacherous instead of beautiful."

I imagined the fights they must have had, the heat of betrayal followed by layers and layers of ice, built into a wall so high, so insurmountable, neither would ever be the same. Questions flipped through my mind, one after the other, acrobats fighting for my attention.

Why, why, why?

Why would he do that?

Why would he look at his little girl and choose to believe she didn't belong?

Maybe it was easier for him to deal with his resentment of her if he didn't believe she was his. Maybe he truly believed Mom had an affair. Maybe he himself had been cheating and it was easier to blame his wife for their failing marriage. Maybe he needed an excuse to let himself fall into his alcoholic abyss.

Maybe that particular *why* didn't matter.

Maybe there was a more important *why*.

One that I had wanted an answer to for most of my life.

"Why did you stay?"

The question hung in the air between us, swollen after all the years it spent on the tip of my tongue. My brothers and I would whisper it to each other after Dad went on one of his rampages. My sister would sob it into my shoulder while she sat at the edge of the dock.

Why?

Why would a woman so strong, so intelligent and compassionate and kind...

Why would she stay with a husband who became a monster?

"For you kids," she replied as she always had, but the answer wasn't enough. Not this time.

"But couldn't you see he was killing us? He was toxic, Mom, and all of us, *all of us,* are covered in the scars he left behind."

She sat back in her chair and regarded me with deep sadness. It tugged at her mouth. The corners of her eyes. It perched on her shoulders and pressed on her chest. Something told me I was seeing all of her for the first time.

"Imagine what a man like that would do if he was threatened. Would he turn his back and walk away from his home? His business? Or would he systematically destroy everything? Imagine the custody battle.

Would he have wanted anything to do with Harlow? What would that have done to her if he fought for you boys, but left her behind? And for that matter, what about you and your brothers? Look at what he was capable of when he had everything he wanted and ask yourself what terrible ways he might have warped your minds if I put up a fight. I was stuck between awful choices and made the one I thought would keep my children the safest." She lifted her hands, a tiny movement. "I didn't know what else to do."

"He was wonderful, once," she continued, her gaze faraway, watching memories of a past so distant it barely existed. "When we first fell in love, when this place was little more than a dream. He was the kind of man who deserved devotion. I see that in you, too."

I lifted an eyebrow, waiting for the killing blow. Any comparison between me and Dad lifted my hackles, even when the comparison was kind.

Pride burned through the sorrow on Mom's face. "You stepped into a leadership position in this family as if you were born for it. You helped Caleb start his business. Helped Eli with school. You were there for Harlow when no one else could even get through to her. You were the father figure they deserved."

I ran a hand over my face as I processed the information. Me? A father figure? If that were true, even a little bit, then I needed to start being the kind of man that belonged at the head of this family. I needed to stop wallowing in confusion and regret and start finding the best way to move us forward and bring us back together. As a family, we were stronger when we were together, fighting for a unified goal.

Mom offered a weak smile. "It's obvious you and that...girl...care for each other." It wasn't lost on me that she couldn't bring herself to say Kara's name.

"I think, in any other situation, you would like her."

"I like her in this situation, and that's saying a lot."

I stood, sensing a natural end to the conversation. "I'm sorry, Mom. For..." You having to watch the love of your life disintegrate into a horrible man. For the impossibility of trying to decide what was best for your children. For years of stress and strain and struggle. "...everything."

"I know, son. I know." And with that, she stood and wrapped me in a hug. I bent to bury my face in her hair, breathing in the scent that had been my rock since I was a little boy.

CHAPTER TWENTY-SEVEN

Kara

I needed as much personal power as I could muster to confront Madeline Lockhart, and that meant I needed to be on home ground. Even though I had never once invited her to visit my apartment, she acted put out when I called and asked her to come by. Mom sauntered through the front door forty-five minutes late, scowling at the pictures on the wall and preening in the mirror.

"This place is so you," she said as she perched on the edge of my couch.

She didn't mean it as a compliment, but I took it as one anyway. While she liked lush fabrics that screamed 'rich with money,' I preferred clean lines and simple patterns. I found beauty in pops of color rather than her bold approach, and loved the way I had decorated, especially because she didn't.

"Why haven't I been here yet?" The question was another weapon, one designed to poison me with guilt over not inviting her sooner. Or self-doubt because she never asked for an invitation. Or—most likely—some deadly combination of the two.

It wouldn't work. Not today. Not ever again. "Because you don't care about things that don't have anything to do with you."

Mom scowled at my answer, confused not to have gotten the reaction she wanted. "Well that's just silly, Poopsie. Of course I care." She licked her lips. "Have you heard anything from Wyatt?"

It only made sense for her to jump right to that particular topic. Her nails were chipped and her roots were showing, which could only mean one thing. Mom was running low on money. She would pay her rent late in order to keep a spa appointment.

"I've heard plenty from Wyatt." I gave her a look that told her everything I wanted her to know.

"Oh, don't look so mad." Mom rolled her eyes and adjusted her skirt, before dropping onto my couch with a grimace at the fabric choice. "You know you've wanted that man since the day you saw him. Don't hate me because I gave him the shove you needed."

Because the only thing that ever got my mother's attention was shock and awe, I went in for the kill. "Believe me, I have plenty of other reasons to hate you."

"Kara Madeline Lockhart!" She dropped her jaw. "I am your mother and a guest in your home. I deserve your respect." She gave me a withering look. "I raised you better than that."

She actually hadn't raised me at all. I raised myself and it was time she took a hard look at who I turned out to be. "You are a narcissist and a parasite. You have done nothing but ruin every good thing that ever happened to me, then somehow made me think it was my fault."

"It's not my fault that you're an expert at self-sabotage. You can't blame your failings on me."

"Not all of them. I've made my fair share of mistakes. But if anyone was doing any sabotaging, you were the one pulling the strings and pushing the buttons." I unleashed the story of my life with her, from my perspective. She blinked in shock at my words, at all the awful things she ever said or did lined up and presented for her evaluation.

"I had no idea you saw me that way...I mean...*wow*..." She frowned, trying to look sad—even managed a tear or two—but I saw it all for the act it was.

"Of course you didn't. You'd have to take an honest look at yourself for that to happen."

"Wow..." Mom sat back, already in the process of erasing everything she just heard. If she didn't remember, she didn't have to take any of it to heart. I could go on being her disaster of a daughter and she could keep being the hero of her story.

It was time for me to become my own hero. I had leaned on Brooke and Wyatt for too long. It was time to cut this woman out of my life, to cut out the cancer before it could grow big enough to eat me up from the inside out. As I stood in front of her, saying all the things I had bottled up for far too long, strength poured into me. I wasn't broken. I wasn't ruined. I would rise from these ashes and become whatever the hell I wanted to be.

"I just thought you should know," I said. "If you say one thing to the press about the Huttons, about those lies you made up about Wyatt and me, I will come out with my own story." I stood taller, emboldened as truth poured out of me. "I will drag your name through the mud, and I won't even have to lie to make you look bad."

"So?" Mom scoffed, frowning. "Why do I care what the press thinks of me? I don't have a business that will crumble under the scrutiny."

But she did. Her lifestyle was nothing but a business transaction and it said a lot that she didn't realize what she really was.

I folded my arms over my chest. "If your face and this story end up smeared all over the news, if the whole world knows you're a gold digger and a black-mailer, think about how hard it would be to find another rich boyfriend willing to take a chance on you. You're not exactly getting any younger."

"Kara..." Mom stood, looking more rattled than I had ever seen her, and risked a glance in the mirror, her fingers fluttering to the nest of wrinkles at her eyes. "What do you expect me to do? They're going to kick me out of the condo if I don't pay them."

"I don't know. Maybe actually get a job and earn your lifestyle for yourself instead of using your daughter and blackmailing good people?"

She dropped back to the couch. "God," she said, covering her face with her hands. "I miss Burke so much."

I didn't know what to do with that statement and barked a laugh. "You mean you miss his money."

"No." She looked at me, her face open and raw. "I miss *him*. We loved each other, in our way. He never wanted me to be anything other than what I was. And all I wanted from him was..."

"His money."

"No. That wasn't all I wanted from him. Yes, he

supported us. *Us*, Kara. Don't you forget that. But he made me laugh. He made me feel beautiful. He made me feel like I mattered. Your own father ran away the moment he heard about you. But Burke? He smiled when he learned I had a little girl and I swear, the way he loved you made me love him even more. That man stared at you like the sun rose and set in your eyes. It broke my heart that you never had that before. Then I saw the way Wyatt looked at you, and it was the same."

Such a display of emotion from this woman should have had my radar going crazy, except this time, nothing about my mother seemed faked or forced. Her words seemed genuine, and I didn't know what to do with that.

"If that's true," I said cautiously, "if you think Wyatt loves me, then why are you doing everything in your power to ruin us? Can't you see how hard it will be for him to trust me after what you did? How hard it is for *me* to trust *him*?" I was in dangerous territory. Talking to her like she was a rational person never ended well. The only thing to expect from crazy, was more crazy.

Mom lifted her head from her hands, genuinely upset. "I did what I did because Burke told me to. He told me it was clear you two were falling in love and I should do everything I could to make sure you ended up together."

I clutched at a chair for support as the revelation weakened my knees. "Are you kidding me? Burke told you to threaten his own family to make his son marry me?" I had never heard anything so... so...*hateful*.

"Well, no. Not exactly." Mom dabbed her fingers under her eyes, wiping away tears. "Burke told me to make sure you two ended up together, that you were good for each other. I'm sure he wanted you guys to do it on your own, but this was the best way to make sure it happened. It was the least I could do, to follow through on the last thing he ever asked me."

And there it was. The craziness I knew to expect. "Don't you see how messed up this is? Don't you see that this isn't how you build a relationship? How do you expect us to ever trust each other if the whole thing is built on deceit and betrayal?"

A deeper part of me wondered if this story was still another lie. Did Burke really want Wyatt and me to end up together? Did Mom really think she was following through on his wishes? Or was this one last ploy to get at his money?

Mom scowled at me, lifting her chin and covering up that brief flash of true emotion. "I don't know, Kara. From where I'm sitting, it looks like you have Wyatt right where you want him. No matter what happens, whether he loves you or not, you're going to get him and end up with a very comfortable life. And isn't that what you've always wanted?"

It wasn't what I had always wanted. In fact, it was the very opposite of what the way I set out to live. Leave it to Mom to transfer her own life goals onto me, as if I never existed as a separate entity from her.

I always knew my mom was crazy. That she wasn't like other moms. But right then, with her standing in my living room, I finally saw how deep her sickness ran. The sooner she was out of my life completely, the better.

Wyatt

I paused by Kara's front door as raised voices sounded from inside. I heard Kara, and though her voice was too muffled for me to make out, she sounded upset. I lifted my fist to knock, but the response caught me off guard.

Madeline's voice, low and too calm. "I don't know, Kara. From where I'm sitting, it looks like you have Wyatt right where you want him. No matter what happens, whether he loves you or not, you're going to get him and end up with a very comfortable life. And isn't that what you've always wanted?"

My stomach dropped at the words.

She had me right where she wanted me?

What in the world was that supposed to mean? Had I been wrong about Kara? Had she been manipulating me this whole time? Had everything she said to me been a ploy to get me to marry her so she and her dirt-bag mother could continue benefitting from my family's money?

I was tired of getting sucker-punched and this one hit me right in the gut. *No matter what happens, whether he loves you or not, you're going to get him and end up with a very comfortable life.*

What the hell was that supposed to mean?

Kara called me her rock, but what if I had been right that night?

What if I wasn't her rock? What if I was her mark?

And what if I fell for all of it, hook, line, and sinker?

CHAPTER TWENTY-EIGHT

WYATT

I couldn't be there. Not with anger and confusion spiraling into a macabre dance, frantic, laughing wildly, and ever more out of control. I needed to leave and come back when I was calm, so I could ask questions and get answers like a rational man who knew Madeline Lockhart was a horrible woman, but her daughter was not. Unfortunately, good timing was not in the cards that night. Just as I stepped off the porch, the front door opened.

"Well, if it isn't Wyatt Hutton." Madeline looked like she had been crying, but nothing about her could be taken at face value.

Just like her daughter, whispered the devil on my shoulder.

"Wyatt?" Kara's voice sounded from deeper in the apartment, trembling slightly and wrapped in anxiety. She was probably nervous over the possibility that I heard what they were talking about, and rightfully so. Oh, I heard alright. I heard enough to set my teeth on edge and my head spinning in circles.

She was using you...

Just like your father used you...

And you were too dumb to notice, even when it was right in front of your face...

Because you always do the right thing, even when it's stupid...

Madeline stormed off without saying goodbye and somehow I found myself inside Kara's apartment. Without thinking, I crossed the room to her and kissed her deeply, my own quiet goodbye. I needed to leave. My mood was swelling and seething inside me, anger feeding confusion feeding anger, round and round until this giant ball of darkness threatened to consume me. But she smelled so good. And she melted into me, her lips parting with a moan that went straight to my dick.

What I felt for this woman went beyond love. Beyond hate. She was every good and bad thing that ever happened to me, wrapped up into one indecipherable package. No matter how much time I put between us, how much she used me, she had a space in my heart and would for the rest of my life.

She told me I was her everything, but it was a lie. She saw what she wanted in me and found a way to take it, to work her way into my heart, knocking over everything in her path. My life was a disaster and my heart was breaking and every time I felt that way throughout the history of my life, *she* was there.

I wanted it all to come to an end and for sanity to rule again. I wanted to be done with the secrets. The lies. The manipulations. I wanted to know that I had everything under control instead of watching it fall to pieces time and again. I wanted to know, with complete and utter certainty, that Kara was real and honest and true. And the terrible reality of things meant that I never could.

Because of the way we came together...

Because of my father and her mother...

Our lives were a constant question mark. How could I ever have faith that what she said she felt for me was real? After what Madeline said in the office, and after what I heard this evening, there would always be a voice in the back of my head, picking away at my confidence and damn if I hadn't lived that way for too long. How could we build a relationship that grew into something healthy and strong when the foundation was weak? The doubt my father had in my mother was enough to ruin him, and the rot spread to the entire family. I wouldn't, I *couldn't* make choices that would turn my life into a repeat performance of theirs.

I glared at Kara, so angry I had no words as I stalked back toward the door, ready to leave before I ruined everything. Kara made a face, grabbing my wrist and turning me to face her.

"Uhh, you gonna say anything, big guy?"

The hurt in her eyes added to the hate in my heart. The swirling ball of darkness expanded, and, like water breaking past a dam, surged through me, carrying away any semblance of rationality. I was nothing but pain. Consumed by regret. Her siren call had lured me in and I was dashed on the rocks at her feet, broken, battered, and barely recognizable as the kind of man I thought I was.

And with all that swirling around my heart, I turned to her and she flinched at what she saw on my face.

I said the first thing that came to mind, the worst thing I could have said. "I always knew you were just like your mom."

The words were sweet, but so was cyanide. And they went about doing their job just as quickly.

CHAPTER TWENTY-NINE

KARA

Wyatt's words landed hard. "Excuse me?" I recoiled, adding at least three extra question marks to my voice.

He turned his back to me, his shoulders rounded and pulled up close to his chin. His breath came quickly and all I felt from him was the white-hot heat of rage. "I heard everything." There was so much malice in his tone that tension climbed up my spine, hand over hand until it could whisper in my ear.

Your mom. He heard your mom and now he finally believes you're just like her.

His words were a bucket of cold water, dousing the flames of my love. The fact that he still couldn't trust me had bile rising in my throat.

"You know what, Wyatt? This is the second time you've come to my apartment and gotten all up in my face over something you *heard*. If you don't trust me, fine. But stop pretending like you do. And never, *ever*, treat me like this again."

Wyatt continued as if I had never spoken. "I came here to tell you I talked to my mom. That it was actually really good. That things were finally starting to fall into place. I wanted to take you to dinner and then come back here and fuck you sweet and slow because for one brief moment, everything felt alright."

I held out my hands, questioning. "Then what the hell happened? Because let me tell you, big guy, none of this feels right." Fear trailed cold fingers along my neck. How could we come back from this? How could we survive if this was all it took to shake us to pieces?

"I heard you." Wyatt bit off each word as his gaze darkened, clouds covering the sun, the low rumble of something terrible in the distance. My stomach flipped and flopped and my heart acknowledged the tremors signifying the onslaught of a catastrophe.

"You heard what? Jesus, Wyatt! Stop repeating yourself and tell me what the hell is going on!"

"I heard your mother say that you have me right where you want me. That it doesn't matter if I love you or not, you'll end up with everything you always wanted." Wyatt crossed his arms over his chest. "Does that sound about right? Ring any bells for you?"

My heart sank. That statement sounded terrible out of context, but that wasn't what had me feeling so desolate. It was the fact that Wyatt was willing to jump to conclusions about my character, based on nothing more than something he overheard.

"Yep." I frowned, crossing my own arms over my chest. "She definitely said that." My words were a gauntlet thrown between us.

The look on Wyatt's face was ugly. "And I'm sure you have the perfect explanation to make it all sound completely innocent. Let me hear you talk your way out of this one, Kara."

I shook my head. "Get out."

His brows hit his hairline. "Excuse me?"

"I said, get out. Of my apartment. Of my life." Of my heart, I thought but didn't say. "I want nothing to do with you. Not one damn thing. If you can't trust me enough to know that my mom is the crazy, manipulative bitch, not me, then you are stupider than I thought. And if you're willing to treat me..." I started trembling, my treacherous chin wobbling, but I swallowed that emotion down and buried it deep. "To treat me the way you just treated me, you don't deserve to be part of my life."

Wyatt had the audacity to look shocked as he stared at me.

"You heard *one thing*!" I shouted. "One thing said by a woman who is known for being awful and you've already cast judgement. Get. Out." I stomped my foot and pointed at the door.

Wyatt ran his hands into his hair, groaning as he tugged, but wouldn't move or speak. Just when I thought he was finally going to say something, he dropped his hands to his sides, turned his back, and left.

I ran to the door but didn't open it, rage boiling through me as I pounded a fist against the wall. How dare he! How dare he accuse me of using him? How dare he accuse me of using my body as a weapon? How could I ever forgive him?

The answer was simple. I couldn't. And if I couldn't forgive him, then that could only mean one thing. We were over before we even began.

Tears spilled down my cheeks as I crossed the living room and collapsed onto my couch, curling into a ball and sobbing into a pillow. Years of disappointment poured through me and I gave in to the sorrow, ignoring my phone as it pinged with messages and missed calls.

Let him call.

Let him worry.

Let him realize what a dick he'd been.

Time passed, though I didn't know how much. There was a soft knock on my door, and then, when I didn't answer, another. And another. Finally, I heard my name.

"Kara?"

I recognized Brooke's voice and sat up, wiping my swollen eyes as I opened the front door, then walked away without a word. It was only then that I realized I'd been sitting in the dark. Night had fallen and I didn't even notice.

"Whoa," she said as she took in my appearance. "What happened, babe? Was the conversation with your mom that bad?"

I dropped onto the couch without a word. I wasn't ready to talk about it yet. Explaining what happened would solidify it and I wanted to hold on to the last shred of hope that this night wasn't real. That I was dreaming. That I would wake up any minute, sweating and crying, with Wyatt's warm arms wrapped around me as he whispered reassurances into my ear...

"I've been trying to get a hold of you for hours." Brooke sat next to me, wrapping a protective arm around my shoulder. "At first I thought you needed some space after talking to your mom, but then I started getting worried. You gotta talk to me, Kara."

Reluctantly, I filled her in on what happened with

Wyatt, the awful way he treated me, and how easy it was for him to believe the worst of me. "I thought he was better than that. I thought..." I swallowed back fresh tears. "I don't know what I thought," I said, hiccupping as I dropped my head onto her shoulder.

That was a lie. I knew exactly what I thought. I thought Wyatt loved me and that meant something. I thought he knew I wasn't like my mother, but twice now, he had assumed the worst of me because of her. I thought he and I were something beautiful.

I was wrong. Oh, God, I was so wrong and I hurt more than I thought I could ever hurt.

Brooke rubbed a hand over my back. "I don't even know what to say other than what a dick move."

I barked a laugh. "Such a dick move." My voice cracked on the end of the sentence and I wept.

CHAPTER THIRTY

Wyatt

Doubt snuck in before I even made it home, followed closely by fear, and then a sense of dread that buried my heart in my stomach. Not only had I jumped to conclusions, but I let anger take over and said the one thing I knew would ruin us. I stayed when I knew I needed to leave and lashed out because I was afraid.

At a stoplight, I texted her.

When I got home, I texted her again.

When I got no response, I called her, leaving several crazed voicemails before I considered getting in my car and driving right back to her apartment.

Only, I wasn't calm enough to have a rational discussion and didn't want to make the same mistake twice. I didn't want to fight and as emotional as I was, as emotional as she was sure to be, a fight was inevitable. I needed to make things okay between us because Kara was...well, she was Kara. I sent one last text apologizing for jumping to conclusions and begging her to call me when she was ready to talk.

A day passed.

Then another.

Then a week.

Then two.

Her silence was deafening. Kara was always up for a fight, always ready to prove herself right and point out all the ways I had been wrong about any given situation. Her lack of response was a response in and of itself. We were done and she wanted me to stay away. I promised myself I would give her that, at least.

I focused on work and my family, and tried to find solace there. At first, I expected I would hear from Madeline, ready to push her blackmail agenda now that Kara and I weren't together. There was nothing but silence on that front as well. It was like they never existed. Like the last seven years had been a lie. Like Dad had never called me into his office and brought me in on his secret and now, a huge chunk of my life was missing.

It was everything I always thought I wanted, a life without them in it. But now that I had it, I didn't know how to exist. Kara wasn't just a part of my life, she was my life. She had all of me and everything was gray without her around to light up the darkness.

As time passed, I found myself unable to keep my vow of staying away. I drove by her apartment several times, but her car was never there. Each time I swung into the lot, I swore it would be the last, only it never was. The longer I went without hearing from her, the more fear got the better of me. I had to see her. I had to apologize. She didn't have to accept my apology, but she needed to hear it. I needed to know she was okay, and then, maybe, I could move on.

All I knew about where she worked was that she made jewelry with her friend Brooke, but after only a few internet searches, I had my choices narrowed down to two possible locations. The first one was a bust. I knew it the moment I stepped into the shop because nothing of Kara's spirit was in any of the pieces.

The second one, though...

Kara's signature was all over the place. In the window dressing. The logo. The look of the pieces inside. Strong, direct, stunning.

A tall blonde with curly hair and kind eyes looked up as I walked in. A flash of recognition danced across her face and all the kindness drained from her posture. "We don't serve your kind here."

"My kind?"

"Yeah." She crossed her arms over her chest and leaned against the counter. "Assholes who take advantage of vulnerable women."

I smiled despite myself, admiring her ferocity. "You must be Brooke."

"And you must be fooling yourself."

She had a point, but this visit wasn't about me. "I'm really worried," I said. "Kara isn't returning my calls. Her car hasn't been in the lot outside her apartment in weeks. I'm afraid something's wrong."

"Does it really need pointed out that *you* are the something wrong?" Brooke shook her head, clearly appalled. "Kara looks tough from the outside, but inside? Her heart is like a piece of glass with all these cracks running through it. Doesn't take much more than a flick of your finger to shatter it beyond recognition. And you? You drove a Mack truck through the thing."

I closed my eyes against the truth. "Is she here? Can I at least talk to her?"

"She's not and you can't."

"Look, I'm desperate here. I messed up..."

"Again." Brooke gave me a pointed look.

"Right," I conceded. "I messed up *again*. Can you at least tell me if she's okay or not?"

Brooke frowned. "Let's see. For Kara's entire life,

she's been treated like an afterthought by her mother. Everything Kara ever did, Madeline managed to ruin. Or steal. Or just simply fuck up beyond recognition. Enter the wonderful Wyatt Hutton. A real class act. He swoops in, saving her every time she needs help, slowly but surely working his way into her fragile little heart. And for one painfully brief blip of time, she had everything she wanted. But then, *then*!" Brooke held up a finger. "This guy reveals he doesn't trust her to such a degree that all it takes is one out-of-context statement from that monster of a mother for him to say the one thing she spent her life trying to avoid. Now you tell me. How *okay* do you really think she can be?"

I hung my head, appalled, and Brooke let out a short, cough-like laugh. "Yeah, that look says it all. You messed up, Wyatt. You messed up big time."

Her gaze darted over my shoulder just as the front door opened. I turned, already aware of Kara even though I hadn't even seen her yet, and my heart shattered when I did. She looked pale. And thin. And so very sad.

She froze when she saw me, tears shimmering to life in her eyes. She blinked them away and set her jaw as she locked her gaze on a door in the back of the room. Without a word, she strode past me. "I'll be in the workshop if you need me," she said to Brooke.

"Kara..." I took a step in her direction and she

stopped at the sound of my voice, shoulders raised, posture tense. "Please talk to me. I am so sorry..."

Kara dropped her chin and sighed, slowly shaking her head, then pushed through the door without a word.

CHAPTER THIRTY-ONE

KARA

Seeing Wyatt hurt more than I thought it would, and I had expected it to destroy me. That was why I had been staying with Brooke. I knew that man well enough to know he wouldn't stop at emails, texts, and phone calls. The more time passed without a response from me, the more desperate he would get. He would eventually try to track me down. I had hoped not being home would be enough to deter him.

I should have known better.

When I saw him through the front window of the shop, I could tell by the set of his shoulders he was arguing with Brooke. My instant desire was to burst through the front door and bury myself in his arms, but I couldn't do that. I *wouldn't* do that. I had to train my poor, traitorous heart out of loving him because as it turned out, my initial assessment was right. If Wyatt and I ever got together, we would combust and it would ruin us both. And here we were, ruined.

I considered walking past the store. Putting my head down and hiding around the corner until he went away. But that felt like a betrayal of who I wanted to be and how I wanted to live. I was stronger than that. Had more pride than that. I didn't hide from my problems. I faced them head on.

And so, with my heart in my throat and my stomach in my feet, I pushed through the front door. I would have been okay if he hadn't turned around, but he looked so bad. So hurt. So...broken.

The sight of him put tears in my eyes and it took every ounce of my will to set my gaze on the door in the back and walk past him. Regardless of how badly my heart wanted him, we couldn't survive each other. His voice, when he called to me, sent energy and adrenaline coursing through my body, but no simple apology could repair what was never meant to exist in the first place.

A few minutes later, the door to the workshop creaked open and Brooke poked her head in. "He's gone if you want to come out."

I nodded and let out the breath I didn't know I was holding. "Will it ever get any easier?"

Brooke leaned against the wall. "Will what get any easier? Seeing him?"

"Learning to be happy after him. I thought I found something I didn't actually believe existed. For a second, I believed in love and had hope for a future."

"It'll get easier. I promise. Time will pass and the pain will fade."

"But it won't ever actually be gone, will it? I'll always be missing the part of me that belongs to him."

Brooke nodded and I could see the truth in her eyes. Wyatt would be forever woven through my memories. He was a thread in the tapestry of my life, one I wouldn't be able to remove without unraveling the whole damn thing.

"He looked really bad," Brooke said. "I don't know if you got a good look at him, but I think he's really suffering."

"Good!" My voice cracked with emotion. "Let him suffer. He deserves to, after the way he treated me. He threw us away, because of *her*." I welcomed the flare of anger. It was so much easier to deal with than the grief that threatened to drown me.

Brooke agreed with me, letting her gaze run over my face as if she were assessing me for damage. I wondered what she saw. Did she see how much I hurt? How much I cared? Did she notice the cracks in my confidence? Could she tell how much I wanted to run to Wyatt and lose myself in the comfort of his arms and how much I hated myself for that desire?

"I always thought the two of us would implode if we got together." I offered her a weak smile. "And here we are. Imploded."

"At least you weren't together for years before you figured it out."

Except we were. Wyatt had been a part of my life since I was sixteen. I had grown up, falling in love with him, even as I promised myself that love didn't exist. Brooke knew that; I could see it through the look on her face. She was simply trying to help me find the bright spots in an otherwise horrible situation. I appreciated her efforts, but they were useless. There was nothing good about what had happened between Wyatt and me.

He had my first kiss—a thing I once called beautiful was now tainted.

He was my first lover—a gift I saved for him that ended up cutting me to the bone.

And he was my first love—something I swore I would never give.

Something he would always have.

Something I could never take back.

CHAPTER THIRTY-TWO

WYATT

I did my best not to think about Kara, but she was everywhere. She was in the quiet nights I spent on the back patio—images of her perched on the railing battering my poor aching heart. Her presence permeated the office, a million whispered discussions with Dad echoing off the stoic furniture.

I had been wrong to assume I knew what she and her mother were talking about in her apartment. I had been wrong to jump to conclusions. I had been wrong to cast judgement without asking questions.

When I started helping Burke, I thought I was a good guy doing bad things. Turned out, I wasn't so good after all. Maybe, I was just a bad guy who had fooled himself into thinking he was good. Maybe, I understood my father better than anyone because of all of us, I was the most like him, willing to jump to conclusions and allow fear to ruin something beautiful. The thought was sobering and awful, but I knew it to be true. I also knew I would stop at nothing to burn that part of me out of existence.

A sound in the doorway caught my attention and I looked up from where I sat hunkered in Dad's chair. Lucas leaned against the wall, his hands shoved in his pocket. "You look like shit, little brother."

"That obvious, huh?"

He sauntered into the room, his shoulders square, his chin lifted, and his gaze hard. He took a seat across from me and sat there, glaring with his perfect posture and military training.

I couldn't help but smile. "You're doing that thing again," I said.

Lucas furrowed his brow. "What thing?"

"That thing where you get all intense and glow-ery." I made the statement—a long running joke between us—and for one horrible moment I thought he wouldn't accept it.

But, his mouth curled into a smile and his gaze soft-ened. "Yeah, well, you deserve it."

I nodded and leaned back in my chair, letting a long breath out through my nose. "Probably."

Lucas lowered his gaze. "I keep wondering if all this would have happened if I hadn't joined the Marines." He frowned as he explained how he had battled guilt during basic training because he knew he had abandoned his siblings to deal with Dad. "But then," he said, "you stepped up and I felt confident that you had everything under control. And that was wrong of me."

I bristled at that statement, but Lucas held up a hand, interrupting me before I said anything. "You were only a kid when I left. Hell, I was only a kid when I left, but you are my younger brother and it was a shit thing to do, running away and expecting you to pick up the slack. I should have been the one to protect you from Dad, not the other way around."

"You did what you needed to do, the same way I did. I'm man enough to take responsibility for my actions."

Kara flashed through my mind, her eyes burning with pain as I accused her of being the one thing she never wanted to be...

Could I ever take responsibility for that action?

Lucas lowered his gaze, visibly gathering himself for whatever he had to say next. "The girl...Kara..."

Her name hit me hard, but the distaste in his tone hit me harder. "What about her?"

"It's clear you guys have feelings for each other."

I ran a hand along the back of my neck, trying desperately to get my emotions under control. I didn't know what my brother was getting at, but she was the last thing I wanted to talk about. "It doesn't matter."

"It does matter. I understand you don't get to choose who you fall in love with. I do. But, aren't you afraid that the two of you might be a little complicated? Is she worth it?"

Yes. A hundred times over. Kara was worth everything I went through for her. She was worth so much more than I gave her. And the *lack* of her was destroying me from the inside out.

"Jesus, Luc. It doesn't matter because it's over."

After years of battling my attraction for her...

After years of falling in love so slowly, I didn't even notice it happening...

It was over before it had a chance to breathe.

Lucas nodded. "That's probably for the best."

I glared at him. "It probably is." The words slipped past my lips and I knew they were a lie. I would regret everything that happened between Kara and me for the rest of my life.

In that moment, I knew I couldn't let it end like

this. I couldn't let her fade away, knowing I had so many pieces that belonged to her. She deserved to hear my apology. She deserved a chance to be whole again. And if she wasn't going to give me that chance, I was going to have to fight for it.

CHAPTER THIRTY-THREE

Kara

At some point this week, the shop stopped looking like a jewelry store and started looking like a florist. Bouquets of flowers covered every possible counter space and new ones came every day. Each delivery arrived with a card, with Wyatt's chicken-scratch scrawling across the page. The first couple were innocuous enough.

I'm sorry.

You deserved better.

I miss you.

I hope you're okay.

After those didn't earn him a reply, he upped his game. On each new card, he described a memory of a time we spent together. He told me about the first day he saw me. That he thought I was beautiful and felt guilty for thinking that way because of how young I was. He told me he hated me instantly and could tell I felt the same.

This is a piece of me that belongs to you, he scribbled at the bottom. *And a piece of you that belongs to me.*

The next day's delivery came with a story about how angry he had been when Burke told him to pick me up from jail, but that anger was eclipsed by his need to protect me when I realized I didn't belong there. Again, at the bottom, where the same words...

This is a piece of me that belongs to you. And a piece of you that belongs to me.

He told me about the night he rescued me from Todd Hudgins. How he slept in my chair to make sure I didn't throw up in my sleep. How uncomfortable he was to leave after talking to my mom, even though he knew I was safe in my own bed, in my own home. He told me he knew, then, that I meant more to him than I should. That he was in over his head. That he knew he would be better off to just walk away...but he couldn't.

This is a piece of me that belongs to you. And a piece of you that belongs to me.

After that, he told me he almost chased after me on my seventeenth birthday. That when I showed up at his house after my mom stole my money, he had never been so turned on as he was with me perched on the railing in the rain, my legs wrapped around his waist.

This is a piece of me that belongs to you. And a piece of you that belongs to me.

He told me about the day he got the news about Lucas. How the only thing that sounded strong enough to soothe Wyatt's breaking heart was me. He called me a balm to his soul.

This is a piece of me that belongs to you. And a piece of you that belongs to me.

Over and over.

Again and again.

I never responded. Even when his words touched me so deeply I had to disappear into the workshop to hide my tears, I stayed silent. Each day, a new set of flowers arrived with a new card inscribed with his version of our history. Each day, I learned a little bit more about how he saw me. How deeply he felt for me.

I never felt so beautiful. So wanted. So understood. Wyatt saw me as something precious to cherish and protect...

At least, according to the story he told through his notes...

"You should call him," Brooke said as I struggled to find space for the newest delivery.

I didn't know if I was strong enough to call him.

Nor did I know if I was strong enough to *not* call him.
"Why?"

"Because..." Brooke gestured around the crowded store. "It's obvious he's head over heels for you. Because he messed up...big time...but maybe he deserves a chance to—"

"To what, Brooke? Apologize?"

She bobbed her head as if I was an idiot for asking.

Fatigue settled over me as doubt spun me round and round. I wanted to talk to him, to give him a chance to explain, but every time I got close, I found myself wondering if all of this was my mother's doing. She was, after all, blackmailing him to marry me.

And it was all so exhausting.

I was tired. So tired. Hip deep in a bog of manipulation and deception, moving forward felt damn near impossible. It would be so easy to give up and just sink in, let it creep up to my chest, my chin. To wallow in despair until there was nothing left of me.

For once, I just wanted things to be easy and straightforward. I wanted to be able to take someone's words and actions at face value. I almost said as much to Brooke, but stopped before I did.

How many times had I gone on and on about wishing I had something, while she was right there, where she always was, giving me everything I needed? In this very instant, I wanted to be able to take someone's words and actions at face value and there she was, being honest with me. Nothing she said or did was manipulation. I had always been able to trust her, and I knew without a doubt that would never change. She would always be there for me, just like Wyatt had always been there.

And just like that, a moment of clarity shone through the darkness that had settled over my life. Or maybe it was a moment of stupidity, but I suspected that was the voice of fear offering that suggestion, and fear often masqueraded as wisdom.

If I could be so caught up in my own drama that I could miss something as wonderful as Brooke's friend-ship, maybe, *maybe* that was what happened to Wyatt. Maybe, while he was trying to navigate an already diffi-cult situation, he heard something awful, something that sparked that fear and it blinded him...

Or maybe I was fooling myself...

The urge to talk to Wyatt sung through my veins, lighting up my cells with energy and hope. I explained my thoughts to Brooke, who beamed when I told her what she meant to me. "But what if it's my mom?" I asked. "Pulling his strings? Making him do things when he doesn't care for me at all."

"I don't know, Kara. Ask him? Ask her? Sometimes you have to take a leap of faith. Sometimes, you have to risk getting hurt. I love you so much and I can't watch you live like this anymore. All the fire and spunk I've always admired is gone. It's like I'm watching you die, even though you're still living. You have to do something, because you can't go on like this. I won't let you."

I digested her words, staring at the wealth of flowers, inhaling the heavily perfumed air. For the thousandth time, I wondered what it might mean if everything Wyatt put in those cards was true.

It means he loves you, whispered my heart. *It means he loves you and you're a fool for not responding sooner.*

It means he knows exactly what to say to make you feel that way, whispered my head. *It means he and your mom have been talking and you'd be a fool if you responded now.*

Brooke watched as I walked from bouquet to bouquet, breathing in their scent, rereading the cards. As I rubbed a petal between my fingers, I realized that I had to know. I couldn't spend the rest of my life missing the pieces I gave to him and not know how much of our story was true, and how much was built on a lie.

I hadn't seen my mom since the day I invited her to my apartment two weeks ago. I really wasn't interested in seeing her ever again, but I needed to know if she had anything to do with Wyatt's sudden obsession with floral arrangements. I pulled up in front of our condo, next to her vacant parking space. The lights were off, and the windows looked oddly empty. I climbed out of the car and peered inside. No blinds. No furniture. No Mom.

At some point in the last month she moved without calling to let me know. It was an unusual choice for someone like her. Whatever had caused her change in living arrangements was ripe with the opportunity to guilt trip me back into her life. The fact that she didn't take it plopped a stone of concern into my stomach.

Hoping she still had the same phone number, I shot her a text, then got back in the car and prepared to wait until possibly forever to hear back. Mom never returned a text until it was convenient and for her, I was rarely convenient. To my surprise, she replied before I even got on the road, explaining that she had moved. The information was simple and straightforward and so unlike my mother, I started to worry. I got her new address and permission to stop by, then drove in shock as the quality of the homes dropped with each passing mile.

Finally, I pulled to a stop in front of a rundown apartment building and then checked the address she gave me three times before turning off the engine. As I made my way up the dilapidated walk, my mother swung open the front door and stepped out.

She said nothing, simply offering a weak smile. Her clothes still looked like her, too tight, too young, too much. Her hair was completely blonde again, not even a whisper of a dark root to be seen. Her makeup was on and her nails were polished to perfection. She looked out of place standing on the chipped concrete stoop, to say the least.

I lifted a hand and stopped in front of her. She didn't invite me in. We stood, awkwardly silent while I tried to figure out how to start the conversation. Finally, I settled on, "What's going on?"

Mom lifted a condescending eyebrow. "What? Not a fan of my new home?"

"Not what I said." I didn't want to be rude, but I didn't want to be weak, either. Navigating this new power dynamic between us was uncomfortable.

She dismissed the response with a roll of her eyes and a flip of her hands. "What do you want, Kara?"

I didn't know what to make of her tone. Everything Mom ever did was designed to create a response in me, but in this instance, there was nothing behind her words. I couldn't even begin to guess at her ulterior motive, though I was sure she had one. Madeline Lockhart always had an agenda. "Wyatt's been sending me flowers," I began.

Mom lifted her hands in a so-what gesture. "Congratulations?"

"I wanted to know if it's because of you."

"And why, exactly, would that have anything to do with me?"

I sighed in exasperation. "Come on, Mom. Because of the fact that you were blackmailing him to marry me? Remember that sweet nugget of motherly love?"

Mom lifted her chin and glared down her nose. "I haven't spoken to Wyatt since that night you invited me to your apartment and proceeded to tell me what a terrible person I was. And even then, all I said was hello as we passed."

"Well, I'm sorry to break it to you, but terrible people manipulate and blackmail." I waited for the flare of anger, the indignant rebuttal, only it never came. Suspicion settled over me. "So, what's with the place?"

"This is the only place I could afford." She tossed her hair. "It's only temporary, though. My new boyfriend is leasing me a new condo, but it won't be ready for another couple months."

I bobbed my head and finally got to the point. "And Wyatt?"

Mom's smile darkened. "Believe it or not, your words have the power to hurt. I didn't like hearing what you said about me, but I heard each and every word. I loved Burke. I didn't want to honor his memory by ruining your life."

"I'm not buying it, Mom. You were fine to ruin my life before I threatened to ruin yours..."

"I didn't think I was ruining it." She leaned forward as she spoke, frustration coloring her words. "I thought I was making sure you got what you wanted."

Nothing about this conversation made sense. On one level, I could totally believe that Mom was crazy enough to think she was helping me by blackmailing Wyatt. On the other, my mom was a lot of things, but dumb wasn't one of them. This story she was trying to feed me could be one last twist of the knife to drive guilt deeper into my heart.

Flabbergasted, I tried to find something to say several times before I realized it didn't matter. Whatever reason she had to move here and stop blackmailing the Huttons, I might never know. And that was okay.

"So, the flowers Wyatt's sending me aren't because of you?"

Finally, I saw a hint of the woman I knew. She smiled wickedly as she delivered her final blow. "They aren't because of anything I said *recently*." With that, she went back into her apartment, leaving me to stare after her with more questions than answers.

CHAPTER THIRTY-FOUR

WYATT

Lucas had never looked as happy as he did tonight, laughing with his soon to be wife at their rehearsal dinner. From my perspective, it seemed as if they spent the evening in their own little bubble, only vaguely aware of the rest of us. Cat looked radiant and Lucas seemed thrilled to be in her presence. From where I sat with the rest of my siblings, things pretty much were as they should be for our oldest brother.

Caleb tossed a napkin at Eli, who was sitting next to me. It bounced off his forehead and landed unceremoniously in his mashed potatoes. "What the hell, Moose?" Eli flicked the offending item off his plate and glared.

"Switch seats with me."

Eli shook his head. "Only if you apologize. I wasn't done eating those."

"Then keep eating. It was just a napkin."

"Just a napkin," Eli scoffed and turned to me with a look that said *can you believe this guy?* I offered a smile in return. My two youngest brothers could bicker about anything and I wasn't in the mood to get between them today. After a bit more joking, they switched seats and Caleb leaned in.

"I'm really sorry I jumped to conclusions," he said. "When I heard about everything."

I shook my head as he spoke. "There's no need to apologize. I understand."

"There is a need to apologize. I let my emotions get the better of me and plopped all of Dad's shit on your shoulders. You didn't deserve that."

"It's easy to do." It was, after all, exactly what I had done to Kara.

"Doesn't make it right."

Caleb's urgency reminded me of my own need to apologize to the only woman I had ever truly loved. I would do anything to make things right between us, and I saw that reflected in my brother. "It's all good," I said. "I understand and I'll accept your apology if you'll accept mine."

"Deal." He wrapped an arm around my shoulder

and gave it a squeeze before giving his attention back to Cat and Lucas. "What about that?" he asked, indicating the beaming couple with a jerk of his chin. "You think married with children is in your future?"

I swiped my water off the table and took a drink. "Probably not." I watched Lucas laughing with the love of his life and tried to stay focused on where I was and who I was with, but my mind only had room for Kara.

Every day for the last week and a half, I had sent flowers to her store. While I didn't expect a miracle, I had, at the very least hoped to hear from her. Instead, I got nothing but more silence. For all I knew, the flowers went right into the trash, the cards unread, my apologies unnoticed. I was trying to be patient, but was running out of that particular virtue. Quickly.

"Have you heard from Kara?" Harlow asked, in that way she had of always knowing what I was thinking.

I wanted to know how she knew, but that was a silly question. She always knew. She always had. I shook my head. "Nope," I said and looked for something else to say.

Probably for the best.
Maybe she just needs time.
It'll all work out.
It's fine.
I'm fine.

Everything that came to mind was a lie, so I said nothing and turned my attention back to Lucas and Cat. Eli bobbed his head and sat back in his chair as Harlow frowned in my direction. She wanted to say something, but chose to stay silent. I approved of the decision.

There wasn't anything to say.

I had something special.

I ruined it.

I tried to make it better.

Kara didn't care.

The end.

But, as Cat leaned in close to whisper something in Lucas' ear, I realized I wasn't ready for the end. I wasn't ready to stop fighting for Kara, not until she looked me in the eyes and told me there was no hope.

I pushed my chair back before I even realized I had decided to leave and Harlow smiled at me as I stood. "Go get her, big brother," she said as my brothers shot me questioning looks and I made my way to Lucas to explain.

CHAPTER THIRTY-FIVE

Kara

I left Mom's and drove on auto-pilot back to the shop. It was closed, but Brooke still would be there, cleaning up and tabulating sales, and I needed to talk to her more than anything.

My heart told me to trust Wyatt one last time. My head reminded me that people were awful, and Wyatt was a people, so obviously I would be smart to stay away. And somewhere in between it all, I just wanted to talk to him because I missed him terribly. I was tired of thinking and being rational. Hopeful that Brooke could knock some sense into me, I pulled into the parking lot outside the shop and sighed when I saw the lights were out.

Why, today of all days, did she have to choose to go home early? I inserted my key into the lock, flipped on the lights, then headed straight to the workshop, crossing my fingers that Brooke would be in there.

No such luck.

I sighed and leaned against the wall as I tried to wrap my head around all the things Mom said and didn't say. Up until the very last few moments of our conversation, I could have sworn she had changed. That she had heard what I said and was truly trying to be a better person. But then, that smile...she knew she was giving me an answer about Wyatt that would mess with my head. She knew it, she did it, and it made her happy.

What a mess. The more I tried to think my way through it, the more confused I found myself. The sound of the bells above the front door caught my attention. I had left the lights on and the door unlocked, so obviously someone chose right that moment to come in and buy some jewelry. I shook out my hair and swiped my fingers under my eyes, trying to get myself together enough to face a potential customer.

Painting a smile on my face, I pushed through the door. "I'm sorry, we're closed—" I began, but stopped when I saw who was waiting for me.

Wyatt stood in the middle of the room, looking

handsome in dark slacks and a white, fitted button-down shirt. He stared, mystified, by the sheer amount of flowers taking up every possible inch of free space. His face softened when he met my gaze and he held up his hands as he took a careful step forward. "Please, don't say anything. Just listen, okay?"

The giant lump of desperation in my throat kept me from speaking, but I did manage to nod. Wyatt smiled and the hope on his face unlocked something in my heart.

"I don't deserve your forgiveness," he said. "I understand that. I messed up. Big. Twice. And I also understand that your silence was an answer in and of itself. But you kept the flowers and I'm here, so I might as well make the best of it." He ran his hands into his hair and closed his eyes. "And now I'm rambling, but I'm nervous and I didn't plan to come here tonight. I just..." He looked at me. "I just couldn't *not* come."

He stared at me and anticipation bloomed hot and violent in my stomach. He didn't look like a man trying to manipulate his way into my life. He looked like a man torn to pieces with desperation. He looked exactly like I felt.

"I don't know if any of the cards made sense. I wanted you to know that you're in here, Kara." Wyatt placed a hand to his chest. "You're in there and you have been since the very first moment I laid eyes on you and you will be until long after my time on this earth is done. We are two halves of the same whole, forged through the fires of terrible parents, joined together through time. I am *less* without you. I..." Wyatt closed his eyes. "You are all I want out of this life and I know I lost you. I know you must hate me. But, Kara...I love you." He shook his head and stepped forward, arms extended. "What I feel for you goes beyond love. I am connected to you. I respect you. I..." He hung his head. "I'm sorry for treating you like you're anything less than a miracle."

I stared at him, still trying to process all that he said. My feet begged to run to him. My hands wanted to grasp his face. My lips wanted to press against his. My heart beat a crazy rhythm in my chest and I swallowed hard, looking for anything to say that might make sense.

Wyatt watched me, the space between us seething with so many things that needed said and for once in my damned life, I couldn't speak. Silence took on a life of its own, saying all the wrong things and Wyatt's face fell. He let out a long breath and frowned.

"Anyway," he said. "I just needed you to hear that." Sadness tugged at his face and his shoulders dropped. "I won't bother you again."

My lips parted, my voice catching in my ever-tightening throat.

His gaze traveled over my face, my body. I watched his heart break as he took one step backward, bobbing his head as he forced himself to accept a truth he still wasn't prepared for. Without another word, he turned and reached for the door and finally I found my voice.

"You don't just have a piece of me," I said to his back.

He turned and I gestured around the room. "Your notes. You said you had all these pieces of me." I shook my head. "But you have all of me. Not just bits and pieces. All of me is for you." Tears sprang to my eyes and I took one tentative step forward, desperate to wrap myself in him. Wyatt opened his arms and I rushed into them. He ran his hands through my hair, whispering apologies over and over, again and again.

I pulled back enough to look him in the eyes. "Wyatt? Shut up and kiss me."

CHAPTER THIRTY-SIX

Kara

The thought of spending an evening with Wyatt's family scared the crap out of me. I was a dark spot in their history, even though Wyatt swore I was the brightest light of his life. After six months of dating, and nearly eight years of loving each other, he swore it was time for them to start accepting me as his girl-friend. Intellectually, I agreed, but that didn't stop my heart from pounding its way up my throat as we climbed the steps leading up to the front porch of The Hutton Hotel.

"So, this is where you grew up, huh?" I asked as Wyatt reached for the front door. I had asked the same question the first time we came here, but I was nervous, so that meant my mouth was working.

He nodded, a knowing smile tugging at his features. "This is the place."

I gripped his arm before he could open the door. "Are you sure this is okay?"

"You have every right to be nervous, but I promise you, they're going to love you." Wyatt bent down and pressed a kiss into my forehead. I took a deep breath as he opened the door and stepped over the threshold of The Hut.

Wyatt's mom greeted me with a warm hug. I froze at first, then let the surprise fall to the wayside and wrapped my arms around her. "It's so good to finally meet you under better circumstances," she said and there wasn't one hint that her words were anything but the truth.

Wyatt offered another round of introductions as if this was the first time I had met his family. In a way, it was. The last time I came here, I was the enemy. That wasn't true anymore. He introduced Lucas as Robocop, which set off a long groan from the rest of the Huttons. Wyatt had warned me about Lucas' intensity, but the warning wasn't necessary. The man had the same friendly smile as his younger brother and I liked him instantly. Cat, Lucas' wife, had this way about her that had me feeling immediately at ease. She was bright and airy, the perfect counterpoint to her husband.

Harlow was every bit as beautiful as I remembered her. Eli immediately put a drink in my hand that was so strong, I had to put it aside. And Caleb had softened toward me, wrapping me in a hug as warm as his mother's.

"Easy, Moose," Wyatt said. "I've called dibs on this one. If you want a beautiful woman, you're going to have to find one for yourself."

My nerves faded as the night wore on. The food was good. The conversation was better. And for the first time in my life, I finally felt like I understood the meaning of family.

"Wyatt told me you run a jewelry store?" The question came from Rebecca, Wyatt's mom. She was the complete opposite of my own mother in every possible way. Her love for her children was deep and obvious. Nothing she said had an ulterior motive running underneath it. She was warm and genuine and I felt honored to get to know her.

"That's right," I replied with a smile, hoping she didn't notice what a difficult subject this was for me. Brooke and I had come to the conclusion that we weren't going to be able to keep the doors open any longer. Our lease ran out at the end of this month and we had been searching for more reliable forms of employment.

"And you make your own pieces?" Rebecca's keen eyes settled on mine. They were much like Wyatt's, pale blue and filled with insight.

I nodded. "Yeah. I started out making bracelets when I was younger," I began, holding up my wrist to show the one I wore that evening, "but moved on to necklaces and earrings." Before I knew it, I had slipped the bracelet off and as it made its way around the table, I explained the intricacies of planning the look for each set, how I lost hours as I twined and twisted bits of metal and stone. "I'm so sorry," I said, cutting myself off mid-sentence. "I'm sure you don't care about that much detail."

Wyatt placed his hand on my knee under the table and gave it a squeeze. I leaned into him, thankful for the contact. "I told you she was talented," he said to Rebecca who studied my bracelet with a shrewd eye.

"My son told me about the difficulties you and your friend are having, keeping the shop open. He also told me that the two of you just needed a chance to get more eyes on your work and it would basically sell itself."

I glanced at Wyatt who beamed at me.

"And looking at this piece," she continued, "I agree with him."

Before I knew what was happening, Rebecca offered us a chance to sell our jewelry out of the gift shop at The Hut. "You wouldn't have to worry about the cost of renting a space or paying utilities. I can promise a steady flow of customers and if this any indication of the quality of your work, I can promise that it will sell."

Excitement sent my pulse racing. "I'll have to talk about it with my business partner, Brooke, but I'm sure she'll be as thrilled about this as I am."

The evening felt like a dream come true, to be sitting in this house, with this family—who I spent my childhood stalking online, wondering if their life was as charmed as I imagined. I said as much to Wyatt, who gave me a look I couldn't decipher, his eyes locked on mine as if he had fallen into them.

"Speaking of dreams coming true," he said, then awkwardly cleared his throat so his family fell silent. "I have something else I want to ask you about."

Harlow covered her mouth with her hands, while I stared at Wyatt, my heart pounding its way up my throat.

"I wanted to do this tonight, because I wanted all the people I care about the most to be in the same room when I asked you to be my wife." He slid out of his chair and onto one knee in front of me, digging into his pocket and presenting me with a beautiful diamond solitaire. The cut was simple and elegant and so perfect that I found myself crying.

I slipped out of my own chair to kneel with him, nodding and sobbing as I reached a trembling hand to press against his chest. "You have all of me," I whispered. "You always have, and you always will."

He pressed a hand against mine, then lifted it away to slide the ring into place. "All of me," he agreed as he wrapped me in his arms and his family cheered.

A month later, Wyatt and I quietly got married on a beach in Fiji. Brooke swore she would hate me forever for stealing her chance to be maid of honor, but I knew she understood my reasons. After all the drama and chaos that brought Wyatt and me together, the simplicity of eloping was poetic. We held hands on the beach as waves tickled our bare feet and the wind blew my dress tight against my thighs.

"This is a piece of me that belongs to you," Wyatt said as he slid a thin band into place on my finger. "And a piece of you that belongs to me."

I repeated the line as I slipped his ring over his knuckle, smiling as years of our life together paraded through my mind. Wyatt was a thread in the tapestry of my life, weaving through my memories and reaching out for our future.

He was my rock and I was his everything, two halves of the same whole, and finally, *finally*...

...we were one.

EPILOGUE

Wyatt

I stepped over the threshold into the office, grunting under the weight of a massive desk. "I swear you're making it heavy on purpose," I said to Caleb, who was supposed to have the other end.

"Who? Me?" he asked, a devilish smile lighting up his face. "I'm hurt you would assume something so devious of me."

"Who's assuming?" I grunted and Caleb threw his head back and laughed.

Sunlight streamed through the open windows and my family scurried around, helping to arrange the new furniture. All the dark, dominating pieces my father loved so much were gone because his era was over. I was taking his place and it was time for this room to look like me, not him. We let the light in to chase out his ghost and as the room transformed, so did we.

Kara beamed at me as she helped Harlow hang a painting she did just for this occasion. Dad would roll over in his grave, knowing some of her art was on his wall, but my sister's work was beautiful. It was well past time for her to feel like she belonged here, just as much as the rest of us.

Caleb and I got the desk situated, then I pulled up my chair and sat down. My younger brothers laughed as they bickered. Lucas snuck kisses from Cat when he thought no one was looking. Harlow chatted happily with my wife, and Mom stood in the doorway, a smile on her face and tears glimmering in her eyes. She pressed a hand to her heart when she caught me watching and I grinned.

We were going to be okay, stronger because we were together.

We were Huttons, after all.

That's what we did.

SNEAK   PEEK   OF   CALEB'S   STORY
—BEYOND NOW!

Curious about the third Hutton brother?

Tap here for your free first look at Beyond Now!

Not into sneak peeks? Still want to know when Caleb's story is available? Sign up for my newsletter to stay up to date!

· · ·

Looking for signed books or more information on all things Abby Brooks? Check out my website!

www.abbybrooksfiction.com

WOUNDED SNEAK PEEK

.

CHAPTER ONE

BAILEY

The security guards stationed outside his room smile and stand as I come near. I know they do it out of politeness, but it unnerves me every time. I want to throw up my hands and remind them I'm just me.

Gary, a tall man with one hell of a potbelly, holds up a hand. "Why don't you hold off a beat?"

Just as I open my mouth to ask why, a loud crash sounds from inside the room.

"Damn it, Brent! I am not going back to LA. End of story!" Liam's words come blaring out into the hallway, with the hushed response of Brent—his manager— low, oily, and too quiet to understand, following quickly after.

I give Gary a weary nod and then smile at Josh, a much younger and thinner version of his partner. "Has he been like this all day?" I ask.

Josh lets out a low whistle. "This is an improvement."

Great. Liam is a challenge when he's on good behavior. When he's in a mood? It's just bad all around. "Wish me luck," I say as I prepare myself to enter the lion's den.

"I'll cross my fingers for you." Josh smiles a little too widely, the space between his teeth glaring at me like a jack o'lantern carved by a five-year-old.

"And where the *fuck* is that nurse? I hit the call button an hour ago!"

I cringe. "There's my cue," I whisper, squaring my shoulders and adding steel to my spine before entering the room.

Liam is up and out of bed, the alarm on his IV pump beeping away. "Took you long enough." He glares at me and folds his arms over his chest. "You need to make this machine stop beeping. Now." I can tell by the way his hospital gown flutters at his waist that it's open in the back. Good god. Does the guy have any modesty?

I roll my eyes and bite my tongue as I hit the alarm

mute button. A quick investigation shows me that the cord has been pulled out of the wall. "These things have a really short battery life." I bend to plug the thing back in. "You shouldn't pull the cord out of the wall or the alarm will go off like this," I say, twisting to look him in the face and give him my best *don't mess with me or I'll cut you* look.

Liam sets his jaw and scowls, looking unfortunately sexy despite his shitty attitude. "Yeah, well, I can't sit still anymore because I'm losing my mind in here. That thing's going to have to figure out how to hold its charge longer."

Right. Because that's even a possibility.

I hold my tongue and study Liam. His auburn hair is bleached blond and somehow, even in the hospital, is swept back away from his face and gelled to perfection. Both ears are pierced and he has enough tattoos to make me wonder what exactly he's trying to prove. The bandage covering half his face does very little to take away from his looks, and even I can admit he's gorgeous.

Well, that is, until he opens his mouth and ruins everything.

Keeping it professional, I put on my blandest smile and stare up at him. "Since I'm here, I'll go ahead and check your bandage. Please have a seat, Mr. McGuire. I'll get the things I need and be right back."

He glowers down at me. "I'd prefer to stand."

I stifle a growl. He's such a petulant child. If this is how they treat people out in Los Angeles, I'm more than happy with my simple life here in Ohio.

"And I'd prefer not to have to climb up on a chair to do my job."

He glowers down at me, determined to get his way.

This guy has no idea what he's getting into. I put my hands on my hips and shift my weight back to my heels, lifting my chin to stare him straight in his face. There's no way in hell I'm standing on a stool to change his bandage. If he wants to see which one of us has the widest stubborn streak, I am more than ready to dig in my heels until he backs down.

Brent, the manager from hell, saunters toward us, his hands outstretched as if to avert the war he sees brewing on the horizon. "Come on, Liam. Do you really want to have to wait for this girl—"

"Woman." I glare at Brent.

"Whatever." He waves a manicured hand at me. "Do you really want to wait for her to find a stool?"

"Nope," I say. "I will most definitely not be finding a stool. You'll take a seat so I can do my job and go check on my other patients."

Liam and Brent's jaws drop in unison and I turn on my heel to leave the room. As soon as I'm out of sight, I pause and blow a puff of air out from between my lips.

"He is such a pain in the ass," I say to Gary and Josh.

Josh gives me a thumbs up, a cheesy grin lighting up his face. "You're doing amazing."

The guy means well, but his awkwardness just adds fuel to the fire of frustration in my belly. I return his thumbs up, looking decidedly less enthusiastic than he did, and head off in search of the supplies I need. When I come back into Liam's room, Brent is still talking a mile a minute.

"When that bitch comes back—" He looks my way as I walk in, a greasy smile sliding across his face as if he wasn't just talking about me.

I raise my eyebrows to let him know I heard, but bite my bottom lip to keep in the response that's stomping its way up my throat. They can think whatever they want to think about me as long as I never have to see them again once they check out of the hospital tomorrow.

"Shut up, Brent," says Liam, and for the first time since he was admitted here, I feel like thanking him.

Liam meets my eyes, and, taking extreme care to exaggerate his movements, he grabs his IV stand, turns, and crosses the room to sit in an armchair, stretching the power cord to its limit.

Yes, his hospital gown is open in the back.

No, he's not wearing anything under it.

I am more than certain he thought he'd embarrass me by giving me a view of his admittedly magnificent backside, but he's going to have to try harder than that if he wants to unsettle me. I'm a nurse, for heaven's sake. I see people's butts all the time. If he's looking for a flustered girl with red cheeks, he's looking at the wrong woman.

"Thank you," I say as I come to stand at his side.

Liam stays silent as I pull on a pair of gloves. I pick at the edges of the tape around the gauze and he turns to look at me.

"Eyes front, please." I don't meet his gaze. The last thing I want to do is give him another reason to complain about something.

He flops back in his chair, ripping the bandage from his face with the movement. The thing dangles from my hand and I stare at it in surprise. So much for being gentle.

"See?" he says, flaring his hands and glaring at Brent. "She won't even look at me. Can you think of any other time a female has been this close to me and not lost her fucking head trying to get my attention?"

Being rude back won't get us anywhere, but he's got one more chance to be an ass before I won't be able to keep my mouth shut anymore. I'm strong, but I'm not that strong.

Brent waves a hand in my direction. "She is obviously not in your target demographic." His gaze sweeps over me, assessing and dismissing in one smooth movement. "She's too old and not nearly trendy enough to matter. If I were you, I would take it as a good sign that she's not trying to engage. This is not the kind of girl you're looking for."

I dab antibiotic ointment on his wound, biting the inside of my lip so hard I taste blood. "I'm right here," I mutter.

Liam shakes his head and pulls away from me. "Holy shit, Brent. Do you ever shut the fuck up?"

I lean in with my ointment and Liam waves me away. "They're all going to act this way." His dark eyes flash as he gestures towards me. "You and I both know that my brand is all about sex. The body. The face. No one cares what I sing as long as I look good doing it." He rests his ankle on his knee and looks me full in the face. "Be honest. You can barely stand to look at me. You're not going to like my music as much now that I look like this."

"All I want to do is change your bandage so I can check on my other patients. As your manager suggested, I'm not in your target demographic." I almost tell him I never liked his music in the first place, but I swallow the words. Two wrongs don't make a right and just because he's an ass doesn't give me a reason to be awful in return.

"What the hell happened to you?" Liam stares me right in the face and laughs. "It looks like you swallowed something nasty. Face all screwed up. Nostrils flaring. Not your prettiest look, sweetheart."

So much for being professional.

"First of all," I say, my words carefully carved from ice and stone. "I didn't swallow something nasty, thank you very much. I just get a little sick to my stomach being around you. Second of all, I can barely stand to look at you because you're an asshole. And third of all, I never liked your music. You can rest assured that's not going to change now." I put a finger on his dropped jaw and turn his head towards the wall. "Now, if you'd just keep your face pointed that way, I can get you bandaged up and get out of here."

Liam does not look at the wall like I just asked him to. He brings his gaze right back to me and there's a flash of emotion on his face that I recognize. It's only there for a moment, one tiny little millisecond of feeling, and then it's gone. Whisked away with a sniff of his nose and a shake of his head. But it doesn't matter. I saw it and I recognized it for what it was.

Despair.

Brent goes off like a windup toy, a slew of words sliding from between his overly balmed lips.

"Holy fuck, Brent. Shut up," Liam says without looking away from my face.

Brent does not shut up. "This is ridiculous, Liam." He pinches the bridge of his nose and smooths back his perfectly shaped eyebrows. "I don't know who she thinks she is, saying those things to you, but we'll have you on the first plane to LA as soon as I get my assistant on the phone. And you..." He levels a finger at me. "You can rest assured that I'll have your job for this."

Liam sighs and closes his eyes. When he opens them again, they're trained on mine, and for the first time since he's been here, he looks real. "You might be the first person to ever be honest with me in my whole life."

A million sarcastic remarks want out past my lips. Little caustic things, venomous revenge for every awful thing he's said to me over the last couple weeks. A minute ago, I would have let them fly in a glorious display of self-righteousness. And in all honesty, I'm not convinced he still doesn't deserve a solid dose of the truth. But that look in his eyes. The despair. I can't say any of those things after seeing that.

I finally settle on: "I'm sorry."

"I might be, too," he replies. And then he blinks and the moment's gone. "Now, finish whatever it is you're doing to my face—" he waves a hand over his cheek and turns away from me, "—and get the hell out of here."

"Gladly." I bite off the word, instantly sorry I didn't let my sarcasm fly when I had the chance.

I've never liked Liam McGuire. His music is vapid. Soulless sound designed to showcase his sex appeal. Combine that with the ridiculous headlines smeared across the tabloids—the temper tantrums, the womanizing, the utter asshattery—and you can bet that I've considered him a scourge on this Earth for the better part of a decade. But seeing that despair in his eyes just now? That bothers me. This guy has everything money could possibly buy, a lifestyle that anyone would be crazy not to lust after, and yet he still knows the cold, dark, empty pit of hopelessness. There's something profound there. I'm just too pissed off to dwell on it.

I gather my things and leave the room. Liam and Brent start in on another argument as I pass Gary and Josh, pausing to blow a puff of air past my pursed lips once again. Whatever it is that Liam's dealing with that hurts him like that, I'm sorry for him. I really am. But I sure will be glad when they ship his spoiled ass back to LA.

CHAPTER TWO

BAILEY

"Have you seen him naked yet?" Lexi Stills, my best friend since the first grade, leans forward, resting her elbows on the table in the crowded hospital cafeteria.

"Seen who naked yet?" I ask, feigning confusion.

Lexi purses her cherry-colored lips. "Liam McGuire, you ass." She picks at the crust of her sandwich and pops a bite into her mouth. "You know, the super-famous singer who just happens to have been admitted here at Grayson Memorial."

"Oh yeah. Him." I shrug, playing it cool just to drive her crazy.

"Yeah, *him*." Lexi stops chewing and lifts her eyebrows. "So?"

"So, what?"

"Have you seen him naked?"

Laughing, I sit back in my chair and scrape my spoon around the sides of my yogurt cup. "Nope. No hot nude scenes with famous musicians for me," I say, even though it's kind of a lie.

Liam has a habit of leaving his hospital gown open and I've seen his ass more times than I can count. I just don't feel like opening that particular can of worms with Lexi right now. Of all the fangirls in the world, she might be the fangirliest and I'm not in the mood for the slew of questions that will follow the admission that yes, I have seen his ass, and yes, it really is as magnificent as she thinks it is.

"Don't give up hope." Lexi looks so crushed I almost tell her the truth. Almost. "I think he's staying here one more day," she says. "After that, I bet they ship him right back to Los Angeles for some kind of plastic surgery miracle only someone that rich and famous could afford." She rakes a hand through her honey-blond hair, pulling little wisps back off her face. "It's such a shame. The accident and all that. I wonder what will happen now that he's all scarred up."

"Maybe he'll learn some humility. That man is every bit as bad as the tabloids make him out to be."

Lexi rolls her eyes. "Only you would be immune to the awesomeness that is Liam McGuire." She balls up her napkin and throws it onto the table next to her mostly eaten sandwich.

"So, how's Gabe?" I ask, carefully enunciating my words so she knows I'm changing the topic now and have no intention of letting her change it back. Being Liam McGuire's nurse is bad enough. He doesn't need to become the sole topic of every conversation on top of it.

"That boy is going to be the death of me." She's trying to sound exasperated, but the look of sheer adoration gleaming in her eyes ruins the effect. "He's as hard-headed as he is sweet. Do you know what he said to me yesterday?"

"I haven't the foggiest." Lexi's stories about her five-year-old son Gabe never disappoint.

"He was playing with his truck on the table and then he looks at me, as serious as can be, and says he's going to need me to talk to him before I find a husband because he wants to make sure the guy's truck is good enough for me."

I laugh as we stand and gather our trash. "Sounds like he's already on his way to being more man than boy. A little bossy, a little protective, and interested in his truck above all things."

Lexi lets out a long sigh. "Lord help me," she says, looking towards the ceiling as if expecting an answer.

The hospital cafeteria is busier than I've ever seen it. Ever since word got out that Liam McGuire is holed up here, we've had an influx of oddly difficult to diagnose illnesses and injuries. Phantom pains and coughs that seem way more serious at home than they do once the patients arrive here. There's even paparazzi hanging out at the front doors.

Paparazzi.

In Grayson, Ohio.

They scurry forward like a swarm of ants every time the doors open, cameras flashing madly, calling out Liam McGuire's name like a battle cry. When they discover the infamous pop star isn't coming out to show off his new badass scar and flash his so-charming-it-should-be-patented smile, they collectively groan and retreat as if to lick their wounds and prepare for the next time those doors swing open.

Lexi widens her eyes at me as she throws her trash in the bin. "Can you imagine how much attention you'd get if these people knew you're one of his nurses?"

A little strum of panic tangles up with my lunch and bounces around my stomach. "You keep your mouth shut, you hear me?" Lexi loves the spotlight. Me? No thank you.

"Fine," she says, pouting. "But you're throwing away an opportunity here. This could be your fifteen minutes of fame."

I link arms with my best friend and we saunter out of the cafeteria. "Nah. I'm saving my fifteen minutes for something way better than this."

"You say that now, but I bet when you're old and gray you'll realize you squandered an opportunity here."

"I'm glad to see you have so much faith in me. That you think the best I'm ever going to be is a nurse to some spoiled brat of a pop star."

"I have more faith in you than you have in yourself, you dingbat," Lexi replies as we arrive at the nurse's station.

"Of course, his call light is on." I let out a little growl of frustration. "When *isn't* it on?"

Lexi shakes her head. "You are the only female between the ages of fifteen and one hundred to be upset because she has to spend too much time with Liam McGuire."

"I doubt that," I say before I head down to his room at the end of the hall.

I don't know if it's because he's been famous since he was fourteen and all the attention spoiled him, or if he's just got asshole in his genes, but it only takes a minute or two of being around the guy to get my hackles up. I don't care how good looking he is or how well he can sing, if you're ugly on the inside, you're ugly on the outside.

Although, for as much as I can't stand the guy, there is a small part of me that does feel a little bit sorry for him. A very small part. And just a tiny little bit. I mean, the guy survived an accident that may or may not alter the course of his life. His tour bus swerved off the road just outside of Grayson and rolled over a few times. Everyone survived, although after seeing pictures of the bus, I don't know how. The thing was just a garbled piece of twisted metal and broken glass.

Liam suffered a concussion and a wicked gash that runs from his hairline to his chin that should have taken his eye but didn't. All the doctors keep muttering about how lucky he is, but I don't know if they've really thought it through. For a guy who makes his living off his looks, an injury like that is probably devastating. I don't think I could be human and *not* feel a tiny bit bad for him.

But like I said, just a tiny bit.

Ready for more? Tap here to one-click Wounded!

Books by

ABBY BROOKS

Brookside Romance

Wounded

Inevitably You

This Is Why

Along Comes Trouble

Come Home To Me

Wilde Boys Series with Will Wright

Taking What Is Mine

Claiming What Is Mine

Protecting What Is Mine

Defending What Is Mine

The Moore Family Series

Blown Away (Ian and Juliet)

Carried Away (James and Ellie)

Swept Away (Harry and Willow)

Break Away (Lilah and Cole)

Purely Wicked (Ashley & Jackson)

The London Sisters Series

Love Is Crazy (Dakota & Dominic)

Love Is Beautiful (Chelsea & Max)

Love Is Everything (Maya & Hudson)

Immortal Memories

Immortal Memories Part 1

Immortal Memories Part 2

As Wren Williams

Bad, Bad Prince

Woodsman

ACKNOWLEDGMENTS

Thank you to my husband—you love me enough to tell me when I'm failing, then cheer me on when things start to come together. I love how we are, who I am with you. There is a distinct delineation in my life, the time before you and the time since you. I never want to go back. Thank you for the hours, days, and weeks you've spent with these words, helping me shape this story into what it needed to be. I love you with all that I am.

Thank you to my children. You guys make me feel like a superstar—even when I spend the day in my pajamas, staring like a madwoman at my laptop. I adore you.

Thank you to Joyce, Linda, Jackie, Nickiann, and Candy. Over the years, you've read a lot of my less-than-perfect work. Thank you for diving into weird characters, and strange plots, with unusual choices, then being free with your feedback. My books, these characters, they THRIVE because of you.

Thank you to Sarah Hershman, my agent. I appreciate all the hustle you do for me behind the scenes.

And to Stephanie, Zuul, Darlene, Hazel, Stormi, Elaine, Vanessa, Cynthia, Suzanne, and Fleur. Thank you for your support!

Connect with

ABBY BROOKS

WEBSITE:
www.abbybrooksfiction.com

FACEBOOK:
http://www.facebook.com/abbybrooksauthor

FACEBOOK FAN GROUP:
https://www.facebook.com/
groups/AbbyBrooksBooks/

TWITTER:
http://www.twitter.com/xo_abbybrooks

INSTAGRAM:
http://www.instagram.com/xo_abbybrooks

BOOK+MAIN BITES:
https://bookandmainbites.com/abbybrooks

Want to be one of the first to know about new releases, get exclusive content, and exciting giveaways? Sign up for my newsletter on my website:

www.abbybrooksfiction.com

And, as always, feel free to send me an email at: abby@abbybrooksfiction.com